"Happy New Year," The Man Murmured In Joanna's Ear After Their Kiss.

Suddenly, the spell was broken, and Joanna backed away from him, appalled by what she had done. She had never kissed a perfect stranger. In fact, she hadn't kissed any man in quite some time.

"I have to go now," she said.

He raised a dark eyebrow. "So soon?"

"I need to go home." Joanna turned away from the stranger and headed for a safe haven, beyond his mesmeric pull. She'd only managed a few steps before she paused to take another look.

He watched her with a guarded smile. His hair was so dark and his flawless skin the color of warm caramel. Wearing a muted gray jacket, pants and a black shirt, he stood out among the standard tuxedos.

Joanna hurried through the double doors. In her heart of hearts she knew she would never forget him and the imposing image he cast against the night sky.

She felt more than a little dizzy, but it wasn't the wine having that effect on her. It was the kiss.

It was *him*.

Dear Reader,

In honor of International Women's Day, March 8, celebrate romance, love and the accomplishments of women all over the world by reading six passionate, powerful and provocative new titles from Silhouette Desire.

New York Times bestselling author Sharon Sala leads the Desire lineup with *Amber by Night* (#1495). A shy librarian uses her alter ego to win her lover's heart in a sizzling love story by this beloved MIRA and Intimate Moments author. Next, a pretend affair turns to true passion when a Barone heroine takes on the competition, in *Sleeping with Her Rival* (#1496) by Sheri WhiteFeather, the third title of the compelling DYNASTIES: THE BARONES saga.

A single mom shares a heated kiss with a stranger on New Year's Eve and soon after reencounters him at work, in *Renegade Millionaire* (1497) by Kristi Gold. *Mail-Order Prince in Her Bed* (#1498) by Kathryn Jensen features an Italian nobleman who teaches an American ingenue the language of love, while a city girl and a rancher get together with the help of her elderly aunt, in *The Cowboy Claims His Lady* (#1499) by Meagan McKinney, the latest MATCHED IN MONTANA title. And a contractor searching for his secret son finds love in the arms of the boy's adoptive mother, in *Tangled Sheets, Tangled Lies* (#1500) by brand-new author Julie Hogan, debuting in the Desire line.

Delight in all six of these sexy Silhouette Desire titles this month…and every month.

Enjoy!

Joan Marlow Golan

Joan Marlow Golan
Senior Editor, Silhouette Desire

Renegade Millionaire

KRISTI GOLD

Published by Silhouette Books
America's Publisher of Contemporary Romance

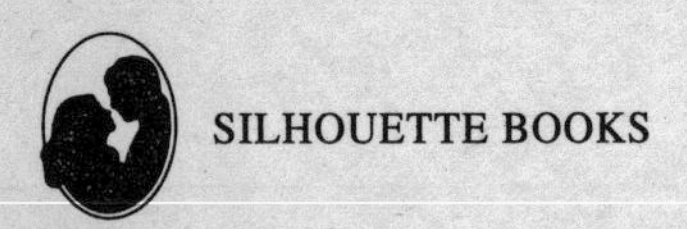

ISBN 0-373-76497-9

RENEGADE MILLIONAIRE

This edition published by arrangement with Harlequin Books S.A.

Visit Silhouette at www.eHarlequin.com

Printed in U.S.A.

Books by Kristi Gold

Silhouette Desire

Cowboy for Keeps #1308
Doctor for Keeps #1320
His Sheltering Arms #1350
Her Ardent Sheikh #1358
**Dr. Dangerous* #1415
**Dr. Desirable* #1421
**Dr. Destiny* #1427
His E-Mail Order Wife #1454
The Sheikh's Bidding #1485
**Renegade Millionaire #1497*

*Marrying an M.D.

KRISTI GOLD

has always believed that love has remarkable healing powers and feels very fortunate to be able to weave stories of romance and commitment. As a bestselling author and Romance Writers of America RITA® Award finalist, she's learned that although accolades are wonderful, the most cherished rewards come from the most unexpected places, namely from personal stories shared by readers. Kristi resides on a ranch in Central Texas with her husband and three children, along with various and sundry livestock. She loves to hear from readers and can be contacted at KGOLDAUTHOR@aol.com or P.O. Box 11292, Robinson, TX 76716.

To Vicky,
for joining me on every step of the
incredible journey

One

Joanna Blake had never been kissed like this before. If only she knew his name.

A few moments ago, he had come to her at the stroke of midnight, an ethereal presence with topaz eyes as enticing as a powerful talisman. She'd been standing in a corner of the hotel's ballroom wearing a borrowed dress, practically unnoticed by most of the medical community in attendance at the New Year's Eve gala. Now she was under the spell of a stranger who had somehow empowered her to be brave and bold, uninhibited.

When he pulled her closer in a solid embrace and deepened the kiss, Joanna's heart rate skyrocketed like the fireworks outside heralding the new year. The sleek glide of his tongue, his heady scent, his arousing heat, called to Joanna on a primal level, a sensual plane she hadn't known existed until now.

He ended the kiss yet kept his sultry gaze fastened on

her face. Joanna was only mildly aware of the room's revelry, the jubilant toasts, the clink of champagne glasses. At the moment, it was as if they were the only two occupants caught in some other dimension.

He brought his lips to her ear and murmured, "Happy New Year," followed by a word that she didn't understand in a language that was as exotic as the man. It sounded musical and mysterious, an endearment, she presumed, or maybe hoped. He smiled and she smiled back, helpless to do anything else.

The spell was suddenly broken when reality took hold. Joanna backed away from him, appalled by what she had done. She had never kissed a perfect stranger. In fact, she hadn't kissed any man in quite some time. Maybe that was why she had allowed it to happen, and so enthusiastically enjoyed it. Still, that was no excuse to carry on the way she had.

Overcome by the need to escape, she muttered, "I have to go now."

He raised a dark eyebrow. "So soon?"

She tried to respond but couldn't quite reclaim her voice. Once again, he had captured her thoughts, her will. She couldn't allow the hold he had on her. "I need to go home." Home to an empty, run-down apartment void of warmth and welcome.

She turned away from the stranger and headed for a safe haven, beyond his mesmeric pull. She'd only managed a few steps before she paused to take another look, as if he still held some mystical power over her. He watched her with a guarded smile, an enigmatic backdrop against the floor-to-ceiling windows.

His dark hair was pulled back at his nape; his flawless skin the color of warm caramel. His attire stood out among the standard tuxedos, a muted gray jacket and slacks and a black shirt secured at the collar by a platinum medallion. The diamond stud in his ear seemed to twinkle in sync with the lights of the San Antonio skyline reflecting from the window at his back.

Struggling with good judgment, Joanna hurried toward the double doors to escape all that magnetism. But in her heart of hearts she knew that she would never forget this event, never forget him and the imposing image he cast against the night sky. Never forget his drugging kiss or that something inexplicable had happened to her normally cautious self.

She reached for the door with one hand and fumbled for the car keys in her small satin bag with the other. In her haste, the purse tipped, spilling its contents. She knelt and quickly scooped up the few items, shoved them back into the bag, then rushed into the corridor.

Once she reached the stairs outside leading to the parking lot, Joanna gripped the railing and paused to catch her breath before making her way to her dilapidated car. She unlocked the door and slid inside, taking another moment to recover. Luckily she'd had only a single glass of champagne, otherwise she probably wouldn't be able to drive. At the moment she felt more than a little dizzy, but it wasn't the wine having that effect on her. It was the kiss. It was *him.*

After fumbling twice with the key, Joanna finally turned the ignition and heard only a grinding noise. She tried once more, and then again, receiving nothing but protest from the temperamental vehicle. The worn-out sedan had chosen that moment to give up, something she'd been expecting—and dreading—for months.

Tapping her forehead against the steering wheel, she released a frustrated groan. Why now? Why tonight? She had no one to call, no one to seek out for a ride unless she returned to the ballroom. If she chose that route then she risked running into the phantom kisser. Maybe that wasn't such a horrible prospect.

Good grief. She certainly didn't need to see him again, no matter how appealing the thought. She already had one male in her life; she didn't need another. Joseph, with his trusting smile and wisdom beyond his years, was her world, her hope, her all. Considering he was only six years old, he posed a lot less trouble than most adult men, especially his father, who had left them alone in the city while he chased after another scheme that promised him riches and excitement. A man who couldn't let go of his youth. Adam hadn't wanted to deal with responsibilities, or a family. Joanna had learned much too late that he would never change.

And now their child—the baby Joanna had wanted so badly—had to depend on her, because his father simply didn't care. If she hadn't been able to send Joseph to live with her mom, she didn't know what she would have done.

If only Joseph could be with her now, but he wasn't, and she should be thankful for that. The broken-down car, her equally broken-down apartment, served as reminders of why her son must continue to live with his grandmother, over five hundred miles away. Although that was best, sending him away had been the most painful experience of her life.

She turned her thoughts to the day when she'd told Joseph goodbye with the promise that they would be together soon. She'd tried so hard not to cry, tried to be strong, but to no avail. Joseph had proved to be much stronger. When she'd hugged him hard, never wanting to let go, he'd patted her back and said, "It's okay,

Mommy. You'll have a good job and make some money, then I'll come back to San Antonio, okay?''

Her little man. And every day since their parting two months ago, Joanna had resisted the urge to send for him so they could be together now.

Joanna had no choice but to put that idea out of her mind. Joseph needed security and a safe place to live, something she couldn't offer until she found better housing, paid off a few more bills. Hopefully they would be reunited soon, if only fate would quit throwing up roadblocks.

The rap on the window startled Joanna so much that she almost cried out. She was overcome with relief when she saw Cassie O'Connor standing outside the car, not some mugger.

She stepped out of the sedan then leaned back against the closed door for support.

Cassie gave a one-handed sweep of her shoulder-length blond hair, her dark eyes reflecting her concern. ''Where did you go in such a hurry?'' Cassie asked.

Joanna willed her pounding heart to slow. ''I have to work at the birthing center tomorrow.''

''That's horrible, working on New Year's.''

The day held little meaning for Joanna, since she would be spending it without her child. ''Babies don't care about holidays. Besides, I've got bills to pay.'' And it looked as though she would have one more debt now that her car refused to run. Just another to add to the pile, thanks to her ex-husband's careless disregard.

''I'm sorry if I scared you,'' Cassie said. ''I was worried something might be wrong when I saw you rush out.''

''Actually, I'm glad you came along. My car won't start.''

Cassie gave her a sympathetic look. "Not a great way to ring in the new year, that's for sure. Do you have a phone to call a mechanic?"

Joanna couldn't afford a cell phone. She could barely afford the pager she was required to carry. "No, and I have no idea who to call." Nor did she know how she was going to pay for the repairs. Under normal circumstances, her nurse's salary was more than decent, but the amount of liabilities Adam had left her with was obscene.

"We'll ask Brendan for a recommendation," Cassie said. "He's bringing the car around. We can give you a ride home."

Joanna didn't relish the thought of the O'Connors seeing her neighborhood. "I'd appreciate that, but you can just drop me off at the clinic. I have some extra clothes there."

"Are you sure you don't want to go home?"

"I'm sure. That way I'll already be at work in the morning, since it looks like I'll be without transportation."

"Okay. If you're sure." Cassie's brassy smile appeared. "And how did you like Dr. Madrid?"

"Dr. Madrid?"

"Yes, Rio Madrid. The man who had you in a lip lock a few minutes ago."

Joanna's face heated to flash-fire proportions. She'd hoped that no one had witnessed her reckless behavior. Obviously she'd made a total fool out of herself with a man. Again. "Oh, him. I guess I didn't realize he was a doctor." She hadn't even known his name.

"As a matter of fact, he assisted Dr. Anderson when the twins were born."

"He's an OB?" Joanna failed to keep the shock from her voice.

"Yes, and I'm surprised you haven't met him before tonight."

Joanna still hadn't officially met him, but she had *kissed* him. "I've only been working at the center for six weeks. I still haven't met all the obstetricians."

"That might be for the best," Cassie said. "He's not too receptive to alternative birth methods."

Classic conservative-doctor attitude, Joanna thought, though the man didn't appear to be typical physician material. But men could be deceptive. She had learned that lesson the hard way. "Hopefully I won't be crossing his path any time soon."

Cassie's grin deepened. "Do you mean personally or professionally?"

"Both."

Cassie rubbed her arms and shivered. "If you say so. Right now let's get out of here. It's pretty nippy tonight and I need to relieve the baby-sitter."

Joanna hadn't noticed the cold, probably because she still battled a slow-burn heat caused by Dr. Rio Madrid. She started to move but realized her dress was caught in the closed door—the dress she had borrowed from Cassie. What other disaster could possibly befall her tonight?

She opened the door and pulled the hem from the car's rusty clutches, immediately noting an ugly smudge of grease on the royal-blue satin. "I'm sorry, Cassie. You were so nice to loan this to me and now I've probably ruined it."

Cassie glanced at the soiled hem. "That's okay, Joanna. I'm sure the dress will be fine after it's cleaned."

Joanna had her doubts about that. ‘‘I’ll get it cleaned for you. It’s the least I can do.’’

‘‘You have enough to worry about. I’ll take care of it. Believe me, with six-month-old twins, you have to have a lot of things cleaned.’’

Joanna thanked her lucky stars that she had met Cassie and her husband, neonatologist Dr. Brendan O’Connor, just after she’d taken the job. Cassie had visited the birthing center and sent several referrals her way through her social work at Memorial. Their friendship made the transition of sending Joseph to live with his grandmother somewhat easier.

Joanna sighed. ‘‘Guess I’m kind of out of it tonight.’’

Cassie grinned again. ‘‘I don’t doubt that one bit. Midnight kisses can do that to a girl.’’

Joanna couldn’t agree more. That kiss was still fresh on her mind—and on her lips. But she was determined to forget it, even though it was the most unforgettable kiss she had ever received.

A kiss delivered by a gorgeous stranger. A beautiful doctor. The very last thing she needed in her life.

Rio Madrid yanked the pager from his lab-coat pocket and pressed the button. Great. A call from the E.R.—just what he needed to end one helluva hectic day.

He tossed the tray filled with his untouched dinner onto the cafeteria conveyor belt and headed down to the emergency room. In the past eighteen hours, he’d delivered three babies, seen an office full of patients and had barely enough time to take a breather, much less eat. He was beginning to question whether he should have hired a partner after Anderson’s retirement. Too late to worry about that now. Besides, he’d always been a loner, and he liked it that way.

After he reached the nurses' station, he used the counter for support. He was too tired for a man barely thirty-three years old. "What's up, Carl?"

The burly nurse glanced up from his charting and hooked a thumb over his shoulder toward the board listings. "We have an OB admit brought in by a nurse from the birthing center."

"Where is she?"

"The patient?"

No, the pope, Rio wanted to say but kept his frustration in check. "Yeah, the patient."

"In Room 3 with the nurse."

"The nurse?"

Carl shrugged. "She won't leave until she knows what's up. Common practice when midwives are involved."

That didn't surprise Rio at all. In fact, he was immediately reminded of his mother.

Forcing himself into action, Rio headed down the corridor and noticed a slight woman dressed in jeans and a sweatshirt standing outside his destination. She studied the toe of her sneaker, her arms folded across her chest.

Although he couldn't make out her features, Rio was hit with a sense of familiarity. Strange, since he was certain they'd never met, but he couldn't escape the belief that he knew her from somewhere.

His steps slowed. Something about her reminded him of another woman standing alone in one corner of a crowded ballroom, seeming as if she'd been trying to blend into the background. But Rio had noticed her immediately. When midnight rolled around, and no one had claimed her for the traditional kiss, he'd spontaneously stepped into the role.

Why he'd done it, he couldn't exactly say. Maybe

because she had seemed so lost and out of place among the medical icons and their wives. Maybe because she'd looked so beautiful yet lonely and he could relate to that. But the way she'd responded to his kiss had made him consider taking her to his bed to welcome in the new year—until she ran away. In truth, she'd been in his bed since that night, if only in his imagination.

He studied this particular woman as he continued forward, doubts creeping in with every step. No way this could be her. He couldn't be that lucky twice. Besides, the woman he'd kissed had been dressed in blue satin, her hair pinned up into a fashionable style, her face carefully made up to suit the occasion, anything but nondescript.

Then the midwife looked up. Dark lashes outlined her vibrant blue eyes devoid of makeup, her fair skin a direct contrast to the dark spiraling curls framing her face. She looked as if she'd stepped right out of a soap commercial, all natural, attractive, appealing in an unpretentious way. Still, he couldn't get past those expressive eyes that now studied him with only mild curiosity, not surprise or anything that would indicate she knew him. But he got the distinct feeling that he did, in fact, know her.

It didn't matter, Rio decided. Tonight he had to play the professional. Tonight he was the obstetrician, and she the midwife. It sure as hell wasn't a good time to get personal, even if it turned out that she happened to be his New Year's temptress. Even if he did have something that belonged to her. Something he'd been carrying around for the past three days, futilely trying to find its owner. And now he was fairly sure he'd found her.

When she didn't acknowledge him, he reached around her, slipped the metal chart from the holder and opened it to check the notes. "Are you with Mrs. Gonzales?"

"Yes, I am."

Rio couldn't help but react to her floral scent, her closeness, the stubborn memories of a kiss that wouldn't get out of his head. He looked up from the chart and met her noncommittal expression. "And you are?"

"Joanna Blake. I'm with the birthing center."

Rio took the hand she offered, noting the smooth texture and how fragile it felt in his palm. "I'm Dr. Madrid." For some reason he was reluctant to let her go.

She pulled her hand from his grasp. "Nice to meet you."

He studied the chart again but couldn't quite focus. The more he looked at her, the more certain he was that this could be his unidentified angel. "Tell me about Mrs. Gonzales."

"She came to the center and presented with excessive vaginal bleeding. She's a gravida 2, para 1, abortus 1."

Rio rubbed his chin. "Three pregnancies and one live birth and this one. What happened with the other pregnancy?"

"First trimester miscarriage about two years ago. This time, she's had an uneventful gestation. No significant problems."

"Well, it looks like she has some now." He flipped the chart closed and held it against his chest. "Did you examine her cervix?"

She frowned. "Of course not. I think we both know that an internal examination could exacerbate her bleeding."

Her adamant tone, the fire in her eyes, intrigued him. Excited him, even. "Just making sure."

Frustration passed over her once-guarded expression. "Dr. Madrid, I'm trained to recognize problematic signs.

That's why I came here with her, to make sure my patient receives the best care."

"I wasn't questioning your judgment."

"Yes, you were."

Actually, he was. He'd seen his share of births go badly in nonhospital settings—one in particular. For that reason, he couldn't seem to stop his concern over nontraditional methods, even though they were becoming readily accepted in the medical community. "Consider me overly cautious, okay? Now do we stand here in the hall and continue our conversation, or do we go see about *our* patient?"

For a second he thought she might smile but it didn't quite take. "Yes. But first I think you should know that Mr. Gonzales knows only a little English and Mrs. Gonzales knows next to none. If you'd like for me to interpret—"

"I can hold my own in the Spanish department, Ms. Blake."

A slight blush stained her porcelain cheeks. "Okay, then." She made a sweeping gesture toward the open door. "After you, Doctor."

He couldn't resist rattling her chain a little. "I would say ladies first, but I'm thinking you might slug me."

"I'm thinking you might be right."

Finally, she smiled, and then he knew for certain. She was the woman who'd marched through his mind for the past three days. The woman who'd run away from him at midnight. His reluctant Cinderella.

Obviously he didn't recognize her. That shouldn't matter to Joanna, but for some reason it did. If she looked at it logically, there was no reason why he should remember. It had been dark in the ballroom, and she'd been dressed up. Still, she couldn't ignore the little twinge of hurt.

But she had to ignore it. Mrs. Gonzales's well-being should be first and foremost in her mind, not Rio Madrid. At least the doctor seemed genuinely concerned for the woman. He spoke in perfect Spanish, his voice gentle and compassionate as he performed the ultrasound.

While he worked, Joanna took the opportunity to study him. He looked much the same as he had that night—darkly handsome, but his suit had been replaced by a blue scrub top that covered faded jeans, and the diamond stud in his earlobe exchanged for a small gold loop. His slick dark hair was still pulled back and secured at his neck, allowing Joanna to look her fill at his face in the glare of fluorescent lights—a chiseled face with a finely honed nose, high cheekbones and a granite jaw. And oh, that mouth. She recalled his soft lips, how gentle and breathtaking that kiss had been.

Her gaze dropped to his strong hands that had pressed against her back, held her close, made her melt. He might not look like a conventional doctor, but he was one fine masterpiece of a man. Even his name sounded striking. *Rio Madrid…*

"Okay, that does it."

The doctor-in-question's declaration forced Joanna back into the situation at hand, and her thoughts back onto her patient. The fear in Mr. and Mrs. Gonzales's faces had lessened until Dr. Madrid began to explain the findings from the ultrasound. Placenta previa, as Joanna had suspected, and now the baby would more than likely have to be delivered by cesarean.

After the doctor was done, he stood and signaled Joanna to follow him into the hallway. Once they were out of the patient's earshot, he said, "Since she's at term, I'll go ahead and do a C-section."

"Bed rest—"

"Is not an option. She's bleeding too much—"

"Dr. Madrid—"

"We need to get that baby out of there. This is the best course—"

"But—"

"—of treatment."

Joanna waited for a few moments to make certain he was finished with his tirade before speaking again. "Just for the record, I'm in total agreement with you."

He frowned. "You are?"

"Yes, I am." She was caught between wanting to shake him and kiss him. Ridiculous, at least the kissing part. "If you'd let me get a word in edgewise, then you might have realized that."

At least he looked contrite, and much too cute. "Sorry. I'm pretty damn tired at the moment."

"That will make one a little cranky."

He sent her a crooked smile. "So you think I'm cranky?"

Cranky, and gorgeous. "Maybe just a little bit."

"Could we settle for mildly out of sorts?"

Joanna couldn't help but smile back. "I suppose we could compromise with out of sorts. As long as we drop the mildly."

His grin deepened and he opened his mouth to speak but before he could, a harried middle-aged woman approached him. "Dr. Madrid, the Gonzaleses have no insurance. I need to make payment arrangements with them. If they can't pay, we need to transfer—"

"She's not going anywhere." His voice brimmed with barely contained anger. "I'm going to do an emergency cesarean in about ten minutes, and her husband's going to be with her. End of conversation.''

''But hospital policy states—''

''I don't give a damn about policy.'' He lowered his voice, his jaw clenched tight. ''I know you're just doing your job, but I don't have time to argue. Have your supervisor call me after the surgery if there's a problem. I'll handle it.''

The woman walked away, shaking her head.

Joanna smiled. ''Bravo, Doctor. I'm impressed.''

His grin came slowly and unexpectedly, but Joanna's reaction was fast and hard to ignore. ''The bureaucracy around here sucks.''

''I have to agree with you on that, too.'' She glanced toward the cubicle. ''Well, I guess I should wish the Gonzaleses luck so you can do your job.''

He rubbed a hand over his shadowed jaw. ''Do you want to scrub in with me?''

Joanna was totally taken aback by the offer. ''I'd love to, if it's okay with the hospital.''

''I'm giving you my permission, and that's good enough. Let's get going.''

After Dr. Madrid had made appropriate arrangements, Joanna followed him to the labor and delivery unit to change. She dressed and scrubbed then found him waiting for her in the operating suite. Stopping at the head of the table, Joanna exchanged a few encouraging words with the nervous couple, then moved past the drape to join the crew at the table.

''I assume you've scrubbed in on one of these before,'' the doctor asked, the scalpel poised in his hands.

''Plenty.''

''You're not doing them at the center, are you?''

That might have made Joanna mad had he not said it

with amusement. ''Not hardly. But I have had several opportunities during my training.'' More than a few in her checkered past. She'd put her career goals on hold when she'd become pregnant her second year of medical school, soon forced to settle back into the role of nurse because of finances. Then later, Adam had completely robbed her of her dreams of becoming a doctor. He had robbed her of a lot more than that.

Joanna tamped down the bite of resentment to watch the obstetrician in action. His skill was apparent with the first cut, his hands deft, his movements flawless as he worked quickly to deliver the baby. Joanna and the doctor smiled at each other in unison when the little girl released a loud cry of protest during her entry into the world outside the womb. A wonderful sound, Joanna thought. She would never get over the miracle of birth, no matter how many times she witnessed it. And from the satisfied look on Dr. Madrid's face, she imagined he felt the same.

Joanna had done little more than observe until he held up the umbilical cord and asked, ''Do you want to cut this?''

''Sure.'' Joanna complied, pleased that he thought to involve her at least this much.

Before handing the baby over to the attending pediatrician, Dr. Madrid held up the infant for the new parents to see and said, ''*Usted tiene una niña hermosa.*''

Joanna couldn't deny that, when she turned from the table to watch the pediatrician examine the child. The baby girl was beautiful with her thick cap of black hair and her round cherub's face. She looked plump and healthy, her coloring good.

Children were truly a blessing, and that concept made Joanna think of her own son and how much she missed him, cherished him. How much sadness had been a part of her life over the past few months without him.

"Ms. Blake, please see Mr. Gonzales to the nursery while I finish up here."

The concern in Dr. Madrid's voice drew Joanna's attention from the infant. "Okay."

As she walked to the head of the table, Joanna noticed the doctor's dark brows drawn down with concentration, and beads of sweat dampening the front of the blue cap covering his head. She heard him give the order for several meds, and other muttered comments from the staff about too much blood.

Something was wrong. Terribly wrong.

Joanna instructed Mr. Gonzales to follow her, trying her best to alleviate his distress with a calm voice. He kissed his wife's cheek, then stood. Once in the hallway, the pediatrician signaled the new father to come with her and they walked away behind the portable crib, leaving Joanna behind, hoping to find out what had gone wrong with Mrs. Gonzales.

Joanna removed her gloves and mask and remained outside the O.R. suite, glancing in the door's window to try to discern the problem. She couldn't see anything for the flurry of activity surrounding the table.

After what seemed like an interminable amount of time, Dr. Madrid backed away from the table, looking relieved. He stopped for a moment and spoke to Mrs. Gonzales, then headed for the exit while the staff prepared to move the patient.

He yanked the gloves off his hands, the mask off his face and raked the cap from his head, tossing them into the refuse container. He then pushed through the double doors to join Joanna outside the room.

"Is she all right?" Joanna asked.

"She had a bleeder, but I've got it under control."

"You didn't have to do a hysterectomy, did you?"

"No. I've managed to save her uterus. They'll give her a couple of units of blood. I'm sure she'll be fine."

"I'm glad. I was worried."

"So was I." He leveled his golden gaze on her. "Do you want to grab some coffee after I make sure Mrs. Gonzales is settled?"

That sounded like a plan, one she didn't dare consider. "I really need to go. I have to call the center then get home. I'll check on Mrs. Gonzales before I leave."

His sultry smile crept in. "Not even one cup of coffee? Just ten minutes of your time?"

"Actually, I'm in a hurry." In a big hurry to get away from those tempting topaz eyes, that drop-dead smile.

His grin deepened. "Are you always in a hurry?"

An odd question. "Most of the time I'm running on full speed. Aren't you?"

"Yeah, but I'm about to give out." He surveyed her face, his gaze zeroing in on her lips before he again locked on her eyes. "Are you sure I can't change your mind?"

Oh, he could, but she wouldn't let him. Joanna started backing down the hall while she slipped the robe away from her shoulders. "I really do need to go."

He watched her the same way he had at the gala before she'd made her escape. The man must have excessive pheromones, she decided. Right now they were working on her in some not too unpleasant ways. Head to toe chills traveled downward and heat settled low in her belly. It would be all too easy to agree to spend more time with him. And all too risky.

"I could walk you to your car," he said through another rogue smile.

Truth was, her car sat in her apartment lot after she'd scraped together enough money to have it towed. She didn't have enough funds to have it fixed, though, and the darn thing still refused to run. She wished she could say the same for her sprinting pulse. "Actually, I'm into mass transit these days. I'm taking the bus home."

"I could give you a ride."

She had no doubt about that. "I'll manage fine."

"Okay, if you're sure. Guess I'll just have my coffee alone."

She forced herself to turn away from him. Away from all the electricity the man emitted like a live wire. She picked up her pace before she changed her mind and went back to him, probably at her own peril.

"Have a nice night, Cinderella."

Joanna stopped dead in her tracks.

Slowly she turned only to find an empty space where he had been. Vanished, like some unearthly presence, into a netherworld.

Joanna laid a hand across her pounding heart and took in several deep breaths. One realization haunted her like a ghost.

He *had* recognized her.

Two

Rio sat once more in the hospital cafeteria, this time with only a cup of black coffee. He didn't dare waste another meal in case he was summoned back to the emergency room or to the labor and delivery floor. It was now nearing 8:00 p.m., and he still had three hours left to take calls before a resident relieved him. Regardless, he was determined to get out of there, even if it meant coming back in.

He should be tired, dead on his feet, but he wasn't, and he had Joanna Blake to thank for that. He'd almost gone after her, waited outside the dressing room and tried again to convince her to join him.

He wasn't sure why he hadn't. Normally, he didn't give up easily where women were concerned, but this woman was different. She sure as hell wasn't his type, surprisingly innocent—except for that mouth of hers. A great mouth, even when she chose to use it as a weapon on him, in every respect. She was also a mom.

Withdrawing the picture from his scrub shirt pocket, Rio studied the young boy he presumed to be Joanna Blake's son. He could be wrong, but he doubted it. The kid had the same eyes, the same dark hair, the same smile. He flipped it over again, as he'd done several times over the past few days.

Joseph Adam, age 3. My heart. Definitely something a mother would write.

Rio had seen the picture fly onto the floor New Year's Eve when Joanna had dropped her bag on the run. But before he could shove his way through the crowd and retrieve the photo in order to return it to her, she had already flown away like a dove finally emancipated from a cage.

He should've given it back to her tonight, but he hadn't. Maybe he viewed it as some connection to her. Maybe he would use it as an excuse to see her again. Maybe even tonight.

Why not? He wasn't one to avoid risks outside his medical practice. Besides, he wanted to know more about her. Wanted to know, if he kissed her again, would he still have the same gut-level reaction? Would it go beyond a kiss? Only one way to find out.

Rio decided it would take her several minutes to dress, make a call, then another fifteen or so to check on Mrs. Gonzales. Only fifteen minutes had passed since he'd left her in the hall. If he hurried and changed into his street clothes, he might catch up to her at the bus stop.

On that thought, he shoved his chair back and went in search of a woman who might not want to be found. Not that he'd let that stop him.

* * *

''Nice night, huh?''

Joanna glanced at the man who'd seated himself on the bus-stop bench where she now waited. She'd been so lost in her thoughts—thoughts of Rio Madrid—she hadn't even noticed his presence until that moment. He was big and beefy, his round ruddy face covered by a full reddish beard. He wore only a faded denim vest—ridiculous considering the cold—his ham-size arms sporting tattoos that ran together in a webwork of blue, covering almost every inch of his skin.

A scruffy scarecrow of a guy wearing a dirty cap and threadbare flannel shirt, his lecherous grin exposing a sparse display of yellowed teeth, stood at the opposing end of the bench. The smell of stale beer and cigarettes carried on the faint January breeze, causing Joanna's empty stomach to pitch.

The big man nodded toward his partner. ''Mind if my friend has a seat?''

Before Joanna could issue a protest, the second man took his place on the other side of her. Wonderful. Flanked by offensive lowlifes.

Focusing straight ahead at the street, she became more than a little wary when in her peripheral vision she noted both of them staring.

''You want a smoke, missy?'' the skinny guy said, his voice rough as unfinished pine.

She hugged her arms closer to her middle and shot him a look of disdain. ''No, thanks.''

The big guy released a grating chuckle. ''Maybe you want to go down the street and have a beer with us. Take a walk on the wild side.''

Not with these animals. ''I don't drink.''

The ogre inched closer, his massive thigh brushing

hers. "Aw, come on now. Everyone needs a drink now and then."

Considering his breath, he'd probably had plenty. She shuddered. "Not me."

He tipped his head close to her shoulder. "You sure are sweet."

Joanna bolted from the bench and faced them, trying hard to hide her fear behind a toughness she didn't feel. "Don't trust appearances, mister. I can be downright mean when I have to be."

The ape snorted. "I bet you can be bad, too." The skinny one let go a round of wheezing chuckles.

Joanna slipped her hand inside her bag, then remembered she hadn't replaced her pepper spray since she'd changed purses the other night. Turning toward the street only enough to keep the pair in her sights, she silently cursed her stupidity for not getting out of there at the first sign of trouble. Where was the darned bus?

Joanna sensed movement, then felt the heavy weight of a huge arm draped around her neck, a hand rubbing her shoulder. Frozen by fear, she stiffened her frame and tried to plan what she should do next. Kick him in the groin and run back to the hospital? The parking lot stood between her and the main building. A big parking lot filled with only a few cars and probably fewer people.

No, she wouldn't run. She wouldn't let them see her fear.

With a sigh, she yanked the man's arm from her shoulder and stepped to one side. "Look, I'm not interested in a beer, or a good time. I'm heading home to my husband who happens to be a cop. So if I were you, I'd keep my hands to myself before I drew back a nub."

"I'd do what the lady says, because if she doesn't take care of you, I will."

Joanna looked from her harassers to Rio Madrid, standing behind the bench, his hands hidden away in the pockets of a black leather jacket, his eyes dark and intense. He looked predatory, ready to pounce.

He came around the bench and put himself between Joanna and the strangers. ''Move on, *amigos.* Find yourself some other woman.''

The ragtag pair faced him. The big one was several inches taller than the doctor and looked just as threatening. ''Maybe we don't want another woman.''

Rio wrapped one arm around Joanna in a protective embrace. She heard a click and realized someone had produced a knife or a switchblade. Her throat constricted, her body stiffened. Then she realized it was the doctor who had the weapon when the giant glanced at Rio's hand that Joanna couldn't see.

The man backed off, looking paranoid. ''Okay. Take her. She ain't that great, anyway.'' He turned away, his partner close on his heels muttering, ''Crazy cop.''

Rio braced his hands on Joanna's shoulders and turned her to face him. ''Are you okay?'' he asked with concern.

''I was handling them just fine.''

''Looks to me like he was doing all the handling.''

''I'm sure he's harmless. He certainly couldn't get away fast enough from you. Then again, maybe it was the knife.''

Rio dropped his hands and produced the weapon in question from his jacket, snapping open the lengthy blade with a click. ''I've had it since I was thirteen. It's dull as dirt, but it looks like it could do some damage.'' He retracted the blade and slipped it back into his pocket.

''Obviously it was convincing enough,'' she said.

"Either that, or he thinks I'm your husband working undercover. He probably has some pot stashed somewhere. So is it true?"

Joanna couldn't help but smile, mainly from relief. "He didn't offer me any pot, just a walk on the wild side."

Rio's smile came halfway, but was no less effective than a complete one. "I meant the thing about your husband being a cop."

"I'm divorced, and no, he wasn't a cop." He wasn't much of anything. "Chances are my ex would've tried to pay those creeps to leave me alone, unless he decided to let them have me." Joanna clamped her mouth shut. She couldn't believe she'd said such a thing. Never had she talked so openly about Adam to anyone. She wasn't inclined to let her bitterness show.

The doctor streaked a hand over his scalp. "Sounds like good riddance on all counts."

She couldn't agree more. She also didn't understand Rio Madrid's sudden appearance, even though she certainly appreciated it. "What are you doing here?"

"I came looking for you, and I'm glad I did."

So was Joanna, but she wouldn't make that admission. "Is something wrong with Mrs. Gonzales?"

"No, she's doing great."

"Then what can I do for you?"

"I thought I'd try to convince you to have that cup of coffee." He studied her for a long moment. "Are you sure you're okay?"

"I'm fine. Really."

"You're shaking."

"I'm cold." She was also lying.

Stripping out of his jacket, he put it around her shoulders. It smelled like leather and the spicy scent that had washed over her sparked her fantasies, that one memorable night in his arms.

"Better?" he asked.

She was somewhat warmer, but not as warm as she'd been when he'd held her close to his side. "Much, but now you're going to be cold."

He rubbed a hand across his chest, covered only by a thin black T-shirt. "Don't worry about me. I'm hot most of the time."

Joanna had no answer for that, at least not a verbal one. Right now she was heating up fast in response.

"I take it you don't own a car," he said.

"I do, but it's at home, broken down." A perfect match for her apartment.

"Then I'll take you home."

At that moment, the bus pulled up to the curb, all squealing brakes and spewing fumes. "That's not necessary. My ride's here."

Rio nodded toward the two thugs now boarding the vehicle. "You really want to do that?"

She looked at the bus, then back at him, unsure of which road to take. "Well, actually…"

He raised his hands, palms forward. "I promise I'll keep my hands on the steering wheel. You'll be safe with me."

Joanna didn't feel at all safe with him, not that he presented a physical threat, or at least the kind that the seedy jerks had posed. But there was something very dangerous about Rio Madrid, the kind of danger that a woman could easily take pleasure in. The kind Joanna would be smart to avoid.

She also didn't like the thought of him seeing where she lived, a crime-ridden neighborhood on the far side of town. But more so, Joanna hated the prospect of getting on the bus with two questionable characters, so she found herself saying, "Yes, if it's not too much trouble."

This time Rio's grin came full force, a sensual explosion. "No trouble at all."

If only Joanna could believe that she wasn't borrowing more trouble with Dr. Rio Madrid.

Rio took the narrow streets slowly, surprised by the place Joanna Blake called home. Not that he hadn't seen its kind before. Every town had one, an area full of lost souls caught in the throes of poverty. Not only had he seen it, he'd lived it until he'd turned fifteen. By that time good fortune had played a part in his future and he'd moved up in the world—a world he'd never quite fit into.

He passed the rows of rickety apartments and small clapboard houses, noting a lot of activity on the streets, and none that looked within the law. Probably a lot of drug deals going down, gunrunning, all kinds of dangerous happenings—things the woman beside him should never have to be exposed to.

He sent a quick glance in Joanna's direction. "Do you live alone?"

She continued to stare straight ahead. "Yes, I do."

He wondered about the boy in the picture. Maybe he'd been wrong. "No kids?"

"Actually, I have a son."

As he'd suspected. "But he doesn't live with you?"

"No."

Rio's curiosity got the best of him. "He lives with his dad?"

"No. He's with my mom in the Texas Panhandle."

"That's a long way from here."

"Yes, but I don't have a choice at the moment."

Rio hated the pain in her voice. "Why not?"

She sighed, an impatient one. "Just look at where I live. It's not fit for most adults, much less a child."

"Then why don't you move in with your mother?" As if that were any of his business.

She shrugged and continued to stare out the windshield. "I wish I could, but I can't. There are almost no job opportunities in my hometown. I have a lot of debts, and working in a larger city gives me more pay. I'm hoping to get back on my feet this year, find a better place to live so I can move my son back here with me." She sat forward and pointed. "Up that next alley. You can park beside my car. It's the ugly white one."

Rio turned the truck up the potholed pavement and to the space next to the car she'd indicated. Behind them sat a brown brick building, three floors high, shutters hanging out of kilter from windows covered by burglar bars. The scraggly lawn was littered with debris and so was the alley, with several old tires stacked against the building among broken beer bottles.

"Welcome to paradise," Joanna said as she opened the door.

Rio got out and encountered something hard beneath his foot. He looked down to find a used syringe under the toe of his boot, thankful he'd stepped on the plastic, not the needle. Kicking it aside, he walked to her car.

"What's wrong with it?" he asked.

She hung back at the front of his truck. "I don't know. It won't turn over."

"Pop the hood."

"What?"

"Pop the hood. I'll take a look."

Reluctantly she withdrew her keys and unlocked the

car door, then slipped inside and tripped the release. Rio lifted the hood but the muted rays coming from the guard light didn't afford him enough illumination.

Joanna joined him at the hood and leaned over the engine beside him. Having her so near didn't help his concentration. "I can't see," he said. "I need a flashlight."

"I don't have one in the car."

Their arms brushed and Rio nearly bumped his head when he straightened. "You should always carry a flashlight. I keep one in the truck."

"I suppose you're always prepared."

He grinned. "Always. With everything." Except he hadn't been prepared for her, especially not his immediate reaction when she stood so close, or his need to kiss her once more. But he wouldn't. Not now.

Glancing over his shoulder at the apartment building, he asked, "Which one is yours?"

"Second floor. Apartment 202."

He braced his hands on the edge of the engine and leaned into them. "Tell you what. You go on up and make some coffee and I'll see if I can tell what's wrong here."

"You really don't have to do that. Besides, I don't have the money to pay you."

He straightened. "You can pay me with some coffee."

"But—"

"No argument. And hurry. I might fall asleep on my feet if I don't get some caffeine soon."

"Okay. I'll bring it down."

"I'll come up and get it."

She looked more than a little worried. "Are you sure?"

"Unless you want me to come up now and check out the place, make sure there aren't any more criminal types waiting for you." Considering the surroundings, Rio realized that might be a real possibility, and he hated the fact that she had to come to this place every night alone.

She started toward the entrance without giving him a second glance. "I'll be fine until you get there."

As Rio watched her walk away, the slight sway of her hips encased in nice-fitting jeans, he realized she was more than fine. And he was in major trouble.

When Joanna heard the knock on the door, she wasn't at all fine. In fact she was nervous over Rio Madrid's arrival. She fumbled with the spoon in her hand, then dropped it into the cup before she made a total mess of her stained and cracked kitchen counter.

Taking a deep breath, she unlocked the door but left the chain intact until she peeked outside. After verifying it was the doctor, she slipped the chain and allowed him entry.

She felt uneasy, self-conscious, when he surveyed the efficiency apartment that consisted of only a small kitchen and dining/living room area that also served as her bedroom. The lone bathroom with its rusty pipes and chipped tile could barely qualify as closet-size although her clothes hung on the shower-curtain rail, the only place available.

"It's not much," she said after tolerating the silence for a few more moments.

"I've seen worse." His gaze traveled toward the water-stained ceiling while he noted the sound of an overloud stereo shaking the walls from excessive bass.

"My neighbors like to party," Joanna said.

"Sounds that way." He turned his attention back to her. "How long have you been here?"

"Almost two months." Two months too long.

His took a slow visual excursion down her body. "And you're still in one piece?"

"So far." She could very well come apart at the seams if he didn't stop looking at her that way.

He slipped his hands into his back pockets. "I think I found the problem with your car. There's a loose wire leading to the starter. I'm pretty sure I fixed it."

"That's wonderful news." The man was too amazing for his own good. "Have you always worked on cars?"

"I'm good with my hands."

She had no doubt about that. "I'm glad it's minor. I wasn't sure how I was going to pay for major repairs."

"Don't get your hopes up yet. I still need to make sure I've found the problem. If you'll give me your keys, I'll see if the car starts." He wrapped one hand around his nape and rolled his head on his shoulders. He looked exhausted.

Joanna felt incredibly selfish. "Why don't we have some coffee first? We can check it when you leave."

"Sounds good to me."

She stepped back in the kitchen and took the pan from the stove to pour water into each cup. "I hope instant's okay. It's all I have."

"Do you have a phone?"

She nodded over one shoulder. "Right there on the wall. Help yourself."

He moved into the small space beside her, bringing with him the scent of night air and incense. Turning on the faucet in the kitchen sink, he began washing the grease away from his hands. "I don't want to make a call. I want to make sure you have some way to communicate in case you have trouble."

"Yes, I do, and it works." For now. She was in danger of losing the service if she didn't pay her long-distance bills in a timelier manner. But she wouldn't give up her only means of communication with her child, even if it meant keeping the heat turned off.

While she stirred the coffee, he continued to watch her as he dried his hands on a dish towel. His presence made her wary. As much as she hated to admit it, Joanna was very drawn to Rio Madrid—his heady aura, his dark exotic good looks—though that seemed unwise. But he wasn't the kind of man a woman could easily ignore—even a woman who had no intention of getting involved with anyone.

After he tossed the towel onto the counter, she handed him one steaming mug. "Do you want anything in it?"

"Just more coffee. I like it strong."

"Oh." Joanna couldn't manage anything else when he reached around her to add another spoonful of grounds to the cup, his chest brushing against her shoulder. That simple contact had her knees threatening to dissolve like the three spoonfuls of sugar she'd heaped into her own coffee.

He leaned back against the cabinet. "Are you feeling calmer now after your encounter?"

For a moment she wasn't sure which encounter he spoke of, the pleasant one a moment before or the disgusting bus-stop experience. She sipped her coffee, yet tasted nothing. She needed more sugar, less Rio to distract her. "I'm calmer, but I'm also feeling a little stupid. I should have walked back to the hospital when I first noticed the big one."

"They probably would've followed you."

"Could be. Never trust a man with a tattoo."

He frowned, then his mouth turned up into a world-rocking grin. "Oh, yeah?"

Setting his cup on the cabinet, he faced her and tugged the hem of his shirt from his waistband. Before Joanna could respond, he slipped the shirt over his head, taking the band securing his hair with it. And there he stood, bare-chested and gorgeous, his hair flowing to his shoulders like an ebony waterfall.

Before Joanna could ask just what he thought he was doing, her eyes centered on his chest. Lean muscle defined his torso; a triangular tuft of dark hair covered the space between his nipples. Although she knew better, she couldn't stop her gaze from tracking the path leading to the band on his low-riding jeans that he had managed to unsnap without her noticing. Slowly he lowered his zipper partway, leaving her speechless, excited, unable to move. Then the tattoo came into view.

Below his navel, a black jungle cat horizontally spanned the tight plane of his abdomen, interrupting the trail of masculine hair leading downward. Joanna's mouth dropped open but she snapped it shut to muffle her sharp, indrawn breath. The tattoo looked powerful, provocative, impressive.

When Joanna finally looked up, she found his smile absent and his expression disarming. "Does this make me untrustworthy?" he asked in a low, spellbinding voice.

Her gaze traveled back to the tattoo and she took in the details, while the awareness that he was watching her sent electricity racing along her nerve endings. As far as Joanna was concerned, this particular artwork made him that much more sensual, seductive, mysterious. She had the overwhelming urge to touch it, to see if it was as silky as it looked. She was as drawn to that tattoo as she had been to its owner on New Year's Eve—as she was tonight. Without regard for common sense, she breezed a fingertip across the cat—only to be stopped by the doctor's grip on her wrist.

He released a slow, strained breath. "Normally I might say, 'Feel free to keep touching,' but I'm not sure that's a good idea. Not unless you realize you're stirring up trouble."

Joanna's eyes moved to the obvious bulge below the waistband of his jeans, which were faded to a bleached-out blue in some hard-to-ignore places. Her face flamed from mortification, from totally forgetting herself, forgetting whom she was with, what she was doing. Again.

She dropped her hand to her side but couldn't bring herself to contact his powerful golden gaze. "I'm sorry. It's just that…I don't know. It looks so soft."

"Take my word for it, it's not." His tone was wry, his voice grainy, deep and deadly.

She raised her eyes to his, finding them as enticing as they had been after he'd kissed her that night in the ballroom. Grasping for an innocuous question, she asked, "Is it a panther?"

He looked down at the tattoo. Joanna couldn't seem to stop herself from looking, too. The muscles in his abdomen clenched as he ran one sturdy, square finger along the jungle cat's back, much the same as she had, causing Joanna to shiver. "It's a jaguar. My onen, or so my mother told me."

"Your what?"

He redid his jeans, slipped the shirt over his head and secured his hair back in the band, much to Joanna's disappointment. "Onen. My animal, or the animal assigned to me at birth. My mother was of Mayan descent. She believed in the folklore.''

''So you're Mayan?''

''That and a few other things. Spanish royalty, reportedly a white missionary a couple of generations back. My family has a strong history of forbidden love.''

''Forbidden'' pretty much summed up Joanna's reaction to this man. An enigmatic, unpredictable man who held her imagination captive, kept her fantasies churning and her pulse erratic. ''Where's your mother now?'' she asked, searching for something that might take her mind off his unmistakable aura, his blatant sensuality.

A fleeting sadness passed over his expression. ''She died a few years ago. She was a good woman, a little misguided in her beliefs, but she was charitable to people in need.''

''Like her son?''

His smile crooked the corner of his lips, a decidedly cynical smile. ''Don't peg me wrong, Joanna. I enjoy my success and all that it brings.''

''But you helped the Gonzaleses, knowing they didn't have any insurance and not much money.''

''I do that on occasion, but I still have paying patients. I'm not opposed to making money.''

Exactly something Joanna's ex would have said, only he had been inclined to involve himself in get-rich-quick ploys, not honest work.

The conversation lulled as Rio Madrid continued to scrutinize her with penetrating eyes near the color of a harvest moon, as if he had some need to interpret her feelings, uncover her very soul.

Joanna struggled to come up with more small talk, but she had trouble assembling her thoughts with his steady gaze now on her mouth. At least he hadn't mentioned that night…

"About the other night," he said, as if he'd read her mind.

"The other night?" she repeated, as if she had no idea what he was talking about.

"Yeah, New Year's night. I find it hard to believe you don't remember, because I haven't been able to forget, *querida.*"

She shrugged, trying to affect nonchalance even though both her body and soul reeled in reaction to his declaration and endearment. "I thought maybe you didn't recognize me." She was secretly thrilled that he had.

"I didn't at first, until you smiled." He rubbed his thumb across her bottom lip. "You have a great smile. A great mouth."

Joanna couldn't ignore the tingles produced by his touch or her heart's incessant pounding. "Do you always kiss females you don't know?" she asked, her voice coming out too high.

He moved his palm to cup her cheek the same way he had that night. "Not normally, but you looked like you could've used a little company."

She could use some strength at the moment, a lot of strength, in order to resist his lure. "I'm used to being alone. Not that I didn't appreciate the gesture."

He stroked his thumb back and forth along her jaw, her chin, grazing the corner of her lip with each pass. "Is that all you felt? Gratitude?"

She couldn't begin to describe what she'd felt when he'd kissed her, what she was feeling now with him so close, his hand on her face, his eyes focused on her mouth, her will caught firmly in his grasp.

Then he lowered his head, slowly, slowly, and softly kissed her, no more than a tease, a taunt, but it left Joanna wanting as she'd never wanted before…

The shrill of a siren interrupted the moment. Joanna pulled away from him and walked to the window to survey the scene, as much to catch her breath as out of concern for the familiar activity downstairs. Three patrol cars pulled up at the curb near the front of the building and several armed officers dashed toward the entrance. Nothing she hadn't seen before.

A gentle hand rested on her shoulder. "You're not safe here, Joanna."

She hugged her arms to her chest. "I don't have a choice."

Rio took her arm and turned her to face him. His sultry expression had been replaced by one of unease. "Yes, you do have a choice."

"I promise I don't. I've looked all over the city for another place to live and I can't find anything I can afford."

"Maybe you haven't looked in the right place."

"What do you mean?"

He dropped his hands and took a step back. "This might sound crazy, but you can live with me."

Crazy? Of all the absurd suggestions, this one had to top the list. "I don't think so, Dr. Madrid."

"It's Rio, and let me clarify what I mean. I have an older restored house in a well-established neighborhood. There's a nice room in the third-floor attic. It's pretty big, and comfortable, with a private bath. The lady I bought the house from kept it as her reading room. You'd be comfortable there. And safe."

No matter how tempting the thought, she wouldn't feel safe—at least from an emotional standpoint—living in the same house with Rio Madrid, even if the place were a mansion. He already presented a huge temptation, a threat to her sanity and a menace to her emotions.

Joanna had no intention of getting involved with another man at the moment, even if he was a successful doctor. She had more than enough worries to contend with. "I really appreciate the offer, but I barely know you."

"You know me well enough to realize that I have your best interests at heart."

How could he sound so certain? "Why would you want to do this for me?"

"Because I'm worried about your safety."

She shook her head. "But I hardly have enough money to pay my rent here. My mother lives on a fixed income and I have to send money for my son. I have all these bills, thanks to my ex, and then—"

"You could pay me in other ways, nonmonetarily speaking."

Of all the nerve. "I will not be your—"

"Let me rephrase that. Do you cook?"

The man was frustrating her beyond belief, not to mention making her seriously consider his offer. "I've been known to prepare a meal or two."

"I'd like that every now and then. It beats canned pasta and frozen dinners."

Joanna fought the urge to say yes. Fought the allure of his tempting topaz eyes and renegade's smile. Fought her own needs and desires making themselves known for the first time in ages. She couldn't very well see him on a daily basis and keep all of that need out of the mix.

"Again, I really do appreciate the offer," she said. "But I can't accept."

Reaching into the back pocket of his jeans, he withdrew a photo and handed it to her. "If you won't do it for yourself, then do it for him."

Joanna stared at the picture of Joseph for a long moment, the one she thought she'd lost, shock momentarily robbing her of her voice. "Where did you find it?"

"On the ballroom floor. I saw it fall, but by the time I got to it, you were gone."

Joanna held the snapshot close to her heart, so very thankful for its return. She had many pictures of her son, but this one was her favorite. She met Rio's eyes and found compassion there. "I owe you a lot for this."

"You owe your son, Joanna. He deserves to have his mother safe and secure until you two can be together again. I'm giving you that opportunity."

He was giving her too much food for thought, too much logic. She should resent him for using Joseph to confuse her, but she also knew that what he'd said was true.

She surveyed her son's innocent eyes, his sweet smile, and suddenly felt as though the choice had been made for her.

Joanna raised her eyes to Rio Madrid's, finding herself victim to his charismatic pull, as if he alone held the power to bend her will. Bend her battered heart. She could not, would not, allow that to happen.

"I'll consider your offer, but if I decide to say yes, it will be for my son."

Never for herself.

Three

She hadn't said yes, but she hadn't said no either, the reason why Rio decided to broach the subject again with Joanna Blake first thing this morning, as soon as he could get away from the hospital.

The night before she had allowed him to stay only long enough for the downstairs commotion to end with several young punks being hauled off in police cars. He'd offered to sleep on her couch, only to learn the couch was her bed. That fact hadn't made him rescind the offer, but Joanna had adamantly refused. At least her car had started, and she'd seemed to be grateful for that. He hadn't tried to take advantage of that gratitude by kissing her again. But he'd wanted to. He still did.

More important, her welfare was at stake. Her stubborn pride could get her hurt, or worse. He didn't intend to let that happen, if he could convince her to move in with him.

He also wasn't stupid enough to deny that he wanted her, but he wouldn't push. Once they spent more time together, who knew what might happen? Maybe nothing. Maybe everything.

After making his morning rounds, Rio set off for the birthing center on foot, the weather as crisp and clear as a new dollar bill. He enjoyed the walk past the small family businesses that hadn't been taken over by hospital expansion. Enjoyed the sun on his face, the cool air filling his lungs, the prospect of seeing Joanna Blake again. On that thought, he hastened his steps until he was almost jogging for the last two of the five blocks.

Once he reached the white brick building with the high-pitched roofline, he paused to catch his breath in front of the pillar that read, Edna P. Waterston Birthing Clinic. He wondered about Edna and figured she was probably a midwife or some rich matriarch who wanted something to remember her by. If not for Joanna Blake, he'd never step foot in a place like this. Too many sorry memories to deal with.

Rio entered the glass door, surprised by the pleasant surroundings. The waiting room was warm and comfortable, nice blue-and-green–plaid couches, contemporary art, gleaming hardwood floors with various plants set out here and there. Soft music filtered through overhead speakers, while a few small children played in a toy-filled area under the watchful eyes of their mothers.

He wasn't sure what he'd pictured, but this wasn't it. Maybe he'd expected something more outdated, a throwback to a time and place in his past when standard medical care for pregnant women wasn't always an option. The type of surroundings he'd witnessed as a teenager when he'd helped his mother tend to women who couldn't afford anything but a home birth. Bad memories of unsterile conditions, one very sick mother, his own mother utilizing primitive training passed down to her from previous generations. One dark night when her limited skills had failed her and the young woman in her care.

Rio pushed away the recollections and ignored the curious stares as he strode to the reception desk framed by a large opening unencumbered by glass. A young woman sitting behind the counter sent him a sunny smile. "May I help you?"

He looked over her head and searched behind her toward the hallway to the left, attempting to see if he could spot Joanna. He wasn't successful. "I'm looking for Ms. Blake. Is she in?"

"Yes, sir, she is. Do you have an appointment?"

He considered giving her his name but realized if Joanna knew he'd come to pay her a visit, she might not see him. "It's personal."

"Can I have your name, please?"

Damn.

He sent her his best grin. "It's a surprise visit."

One hand went to her throat, but her smile remained intact. "Well, I'm not sure Joanna would like that kind of surprise."

Rio couldn't argue that. "Just tell her I'm a doctor from Memorial, okay? That's all she needs to know."

She chewed her bottom lip. "I'm not really sure..."

He leaned into the counter and sought out her name from the badge pinned on her lapel. "I'd really appreciate it if you would, Stephanie."

Keeping her eyes locked on Rio, the woman picked up the phone, punched a button and slowly repeated the message. After she hung up, she said, "Wait right here. She'll be with you in a minute." The receptionist stacked a few folders then regarded him again with another smile. "So, what kind of doctor are you?"

"OB."

She leaned a cheek on her palm and gave him a coy look. "Really?"

"Yeah. Really." She was flirting with him. Maybe some other time, Rio might have flirted back. But the only woman he was interested in at the moment had yet to appear.

He heard the familiar sound of Joanna Blake's voice, soft and soothing, deadly as far as he was concerned. Knowing she was nearby had his body reacting in ways not appropriate for a grown man, especially in this setting.

The door to his left opened and a very pregnant woman walked out with Joanna following behind. He immediately recognized the patient. Allison Cartwright, *his* patient.

Rio didn't know who looked more shocked, Allison or Joanna. Both stared at him a long moment, but Allison spoke first. "Hi, Dr. Madrid. Fancy meeting you here."

He couldn't ignore the sudden flash of anger. "Guess I could say the same thing. What are you doing here?"

She raised one shoulder in a shrug. "Now don't get upset. I'm just visiting. Joanna was explaining the center's birthing methods to me."

"No problem," he said, but it was, at least for him. Rio leveled his gaze on Joanna. "Do you have a minute, Ms. Blake?"

"I'm leaving, so she does," Allison answered for her, then hurried out the front door in a matter of seconds.

"What can I do for you, Dr. Madrid?" Joanna's tone was professional, with only a hint of friendliness.

He glanced back over his shoulder at Stephanie, who still continued to stare, then turned his smile on Joanna. ''You don't really want to discuss that here, do you, Ms. Blake?''

Color splashed across Joanna's cheeks as she held open the door leading from the reception area. ''Follow me, but I only have a few minutes.''

''That's all I need,'' he said. ''For now.''

So much for not pushing. If he knew what was best, he'd stop with the innuendo. But for some reason, Joanna Blake unearthed his wicked side, trampled his control.

He followed her down the corridor, watching the gentle sway of her hips encased in black slacks, not jeans, but just as high impact.

''All the exam rooms are full, so this will have to do.'' She stopped at a room set off in another alcove away from the main corridor, stepped to one side and allowed Rio to enter.

The place resembled something straight out of a bed-and-breakfast inn, complete with a queen-size bed, rocking chair and redbrick fireplace. He found the decor to be surprisingly elegant, all flowers and lace, reminding him of his own home's attic room, the one he'd offered to Joanna Blake, the reason why he was here. But first, he had a few other questions for her.

''What was Allison Cartwright doing here?''

''She's considering using the center instead of the hospital.''

''Why?''

''Well, she's still on probation at her new job, so she has no insurance, and she can't really afford the hospital bill.''

''What about the baby's father?''

''She told me he's out of the picture.''

''The same thing she told me.'' His thoughts about Allison began to falter when he homed in on Joanna's mouth. Why the hell couldn't he keep his eyes off her?

Glancing away, he said, ''I'm sure the hospital would be willing to work something out financially. I'd be willing to do the same.''

Joanna frowned. ''That's for her to decide, don't you agree?''

''We'll see,'' he said, thinking he sounded like a jerk. He wasn't necessarily opposed to what Joanna Blake did for a living. He even understood the need in some cases. But he still couldn't get past his concern for babies being born off hospital premises, although he had to admit the place wasn't anything at all like what he'd expected.

He shot a glance at the open door to his right and noticed a whirlpool centered in a large bathroom.

He strolled around the room and stopped at the bed, testing its firmness with a push of his palm. ''What are the rates for this honeymoon suite?''

''For your information, it's the Rose Room, one of our birthing facilities,'' she said, impatience evident in her voice, her rigid frame. ''And our rates are about one-third the cost of standard hospital rooms.''

Her defensive tone made Rio all the more determined to play with her a little, in a figurative sense, at least at the moment. ''Nice bed. Nice place. No stirrups?''

''No stirrups. We don't need them. But we do have ultrasound equipment and fetal monitors, many of those other little medical marvels you find at a hospital.''

He inclined his head toward the bathroom. ''What's the whirlpool for?'' As if he didn't know.

''Water births.''

He rubbed his chin. ''Oh. I thought maybe this doubled as a conception room, too.''

A smile began to form on her lips but soon faded. ''That usually happens before the patient comes to us.''

''Usually? Ah, so someone *has* used this room for a little extracurricular activity.'' He had no trouble picturing that happening—with him and Joanna Blake.

She rolled her eyes to the vaulted ceiling. ''No one's committed any hanky-panky in this room. Not that I'm aware of. At least not me.''

Rio was more than relieved over that admission. He moved to the bathroom's open doorway and stared inside, one hip cocked against the frame. ''I think this room would be better put to use with a bottle of champagne, some candles, and a man and a woman intent on making a baby, not having one.''

''Very amusing, Doctor.''

He faced her again and grinned. ''Do you have something against romance, Ms. Blake?''

''I don't have time for romance. I do have several patients to see, so what do you need?''

Rio sent another pointed look at the bed. When he brought his attention back to her, he noticed she was looking at the same spot, maybe even imagining them on that bed, or some bed, tangled together in sheets, sweat and great sex. Or maybe he was caught in the wishful-thinking trap.

Clearing his throat to gain her attention, he said, ''I don't have a lot of time, either, so I'll get to the point.''

''Hallelujah.''

He ignored her sarcasm and continued. ''I'm here to find out if you've come to a decision yet about moving in with me.''

Her eyes widened, looked panicked. She rushed to the

door and closed it before facing him again. ''Keep your voice down, please. I don't want the staff to think that I'm *moving in* moving in with you.''

''Then you are going to move in with me?''

''I didn't say that.''

''Yeah, you did.''

''What I said was...'' She threaded her bottom lip through her teeth. ''I don't remember what I said.''

He strolled to her, hands jammed in his pockets to keep from touching her even though he really, really wanted to. ''Let me refresh your memory. Last night you said you'd think about it, a minute ago you said yes.''

''I did no such thing.''

He inched a little closer until they were almost touching and braced one hand on the door, above her head. ''Maybe not in so many words, but the message I got was pretty clear. So when do you want to do it?''

Her breath hitched. ''Do what?''

He could think of one particular response to that but decided to give her the proper one. ''Move in with me. How about this weekend?''

Her gaze roamed to his mouth. ''You don't give up easily, do you?''

Not when he wanted something badly enough, and he had to admit he wanted her badly. But she wasn't a catch-me-if-you-can kind of girl, so he damn sure better proceed with caution. ''No, I don't give up easily, especially when a woman's life might be at stake. So is Saturday good for you?''

Indecision warred in her expression. She opened her mouth, shut it, then opened it again. ''Okay, I guess. I'm not on call, so this weekend would be fine.''

''Great. I'm not on call, either.'' His first instinct was to kiss her until both of them struggled for air. He went with his second—a simple smile. "What made you decide?"

"My son."

He expected that, admired it even, but he'd like to think that living with him wouldn't be such a sorry prospect for either one of them. Although, come to think of it, he'd never lived with a woman for more than a weekend. He wasn't sure how he would adjust to having her there all the time, keeping him at arm's length, at least for the time being. But he was more than willing to try it, see where it led.

He stepped back and grinned at her stern features. "Hey, don't look so serious. We might have a good time."

She crossed her arms over her chest and sighed. "I'm not looking for a good time, Dr. Madrid. I'm looking for a safe place to stay. A temporary place to stay."

She said the words with conviction, with heavy emphasis on "temporary." That was fine by Rio. A permanent relationship wasn't something that had remotely entered his mind, regardless of the fact that Joanna Blake seemed the type who deserved something solid and steady. "First rule, call me Rio. Second, you can stay as long as you like. Other than that, there are no rules."

Her smile was hesitant, but had an immediate effect on Rio's suddenly sensitive libido. "With our schedules, you won't even know I'm there," she said.

Unable to help himself, Rio reached out and brushed a curl from her face. He might have serious doubts about how this was going to work, but he had no doubt she wouldn't be easy to ignore.

"Believe me, I'll know you're there."

Joanna had her doubts about moving in with Rio Madrid. But when moving day came, she brought along her few possessions and a whole lot of misgivings. Being near him threatened her common sense, uncovered dormant urges best left hidden away, reminded her that she had very basic feminine needs. Needs she had no business acknowledging. But she had to do this for Joseph.

She kept telling herself that very thing while standing on Rio's front porch, hangers full of clothing draped over her arm, waiting for the doctor—dressed in tattered jeans and black leather jacket—to open the door. Today he'd pulled his hair back on the sides and top, the rest falling to his shoulders. He looked like an A-1 fantasy, a woman's dream. So did his residence.

She'd heard about the King William district, but nothing could compare to witnessing its splendor. The well-kept house resembled an English manor, beautiful and bigger than any home Joanna had lived in during her thirty-four years. Unlike her neighborhood, the area was absent of noisy cars and deafening music. No threatening characters and criminal activity, at least on the surface.

"There's something I forgot to tell you."

The declaration drew Joanna's attention to Rio, his hand on the brass knob, a box tucked underneath his arm. Nothing in his expression gave any indication of what that "something" was.

She backed away from the porch and studied the facade all the way up to the third-story dormers. "Let me guess. You have a commune living here."

"No, but I do have a roommate."

Before Joanna had the chance to unpack, the secrets had already begun. Now she would have to explain to her mother that she was not living with only one man, but two. "You should have told me before I agreed to come here."

"I didn't want to give you any reason to change your mind. Besides, I think you'll like her."

Her? He had a woman living with him? A lover? That shouldn't matter one way or the other to Joanna, but for some reason it did. "Your roommate's female?"

"Yeah, Gabby. She's great." His tone was full of pride and affection.

Joanna tried to mask her shock, hide her frustration with an even tone. "What does she think about me moving in?"

He grinned, his white teeth set off against his warm brown skin. "I haven't told her yet."

That set Joanna's teeth on edge. "You didn't tell her?"

"She wouldn't understand."

Oh, marvelous. What had Joanna gotten herself into? What if this woman refused to let her live here, forcing Joanna to reside in her own car or a seedy motel? "Well then, maybe I should wait out here until you make sure it's okay."

"She won't mind. She's pretty friendly."

"Are you sure you don't want to talk to her first?"

"Nope. Just be prepared for the welcome." Rio pushed open the door and waited for Joanna to move past him.

The roommate was all but forgotten when Joanna stepped inside the circular foyer. The floor's majestic white marble tile glistened like the surface of a frozen pond. A chandelier hanging from the two-story ceiling dripped diamond-like crystals. Straight ahead, a staircase with a black iron banister climbed upward until it took a turn to the left at a large landing. Above that landing, a window set with stained glass shot laser beams of light over the walls and white-carpeted stairs. The panes shaped a black cat with exotic gold eyes. Breathtaking, but almost out of place among the traditional elegance. Joanna continued to stare as if cemented in place by the animal's metallic gaze.

"That's a beautiful window," she said.

"Thanks. I designed it."

She studied Rio Madrid, now facing her at the bottom of the stairs, amazed at how much he resembled the animal, how he possessed the ability to hold her captive with his topaz eyes. Maybe this was Rio Madrid's idea of a self-portrait, because in Joanna's opinion, he, too, contrasted with the environment. Rugged appeal surrounded by refinement.

Danger in the midst of majesty.

Click-clack noises that sounded like hooves drew Joanna's attention to the hallway flowing into the vestibule from her right. Before Joanna could brace herself, a huge black and gray mottled thing came bounding into the foyer, streaking past her to Rio.

"Some watchdog you are." The beast rose on hind legs, massive front paws propped on Rio's chest. "Get down, Gabby."

This was Gabby, the mysterious roommate?

Rio slid the box and dog to the floor then shucked off his jacket and hung it over the banister. He scratched the head of the monstrosity with heavy jowls and pointy ears. "Gabby, this is Joanna. Joanna, my roommate, Gabby."

Joanna wasn't sure whether to be really angry or really relieved. "Very funny. I thought you meant you lived with—"

"A woman. I know, but I wasn't sure how you'd feel about residing with an overgrown lapdog." Rio tried to affect little-boy innocence with a shrug, but it was lost on Joanna due to his toxic smile, the snug fit of his long-sleeved white thermal shirt and soft, washed jeans that molded him in all the right places, leaving no doubt he was all man.

She looked down at the dog, whose tongue hung out one side of her mouth, her head cocked as if totally enthralled by her master. Joanna couldn't blame her. The doctor made her want to pant and fawn, but she sure as heck wouldn't do that.

Joanna clutched the hangers to her chest when Gabby cautiously moved to sniff her feet. At least the dog's tail was wagging, a good thing, Joanna decided, considering the size of the canine's teeth.

Uncertain what to do next, Joanna said, "Hey, Gabby."

As if totally disinterested in Joanna's greeting, the dog turned her attention back to her master with a look that could best be described as love-struck.

"I found her on the side of the road about three years ago," Rio said, scratching Gabby behind the ears. "She was starved, I think maybe even beaten. It took me a year to get her to trust me and not to cower."

Obviously Rio Madrid made it a habit to pick up distressed females. "She looks healthy now. And big."

"She's a big baby." Rio pointed at the floor. "Stay." Gabby tucked her tail between her legs and stretched out on the black Oriental rug at the foot of the stairs, her head resting on crossed paws.

Joanna suspected that many females, regardless of their species, would gladly drop to the ground in answer to his command. Not this female. Joanna was stronger than that. At least she hoped so, although at times she greatly questioned her strength in his presence. Especially now.

Rio gestured toward the staircase. "You, Ms. Blake, may come with me."

Joanna silently followed behind him trying hard to avert her gaze from the roll of his narrow hips as he took the stairs with a long stride. Even when they arrived on the second floor, she couldn't seem to stop looking, imagining, remembering the night he'd kissed her, the night he'd taken off his shirt at her apartment. And that tattoo. Below that tattoo…

"My bedroom's down there." Rio pointed to his left.

"Really?" Joanna's voice sounded high-pitched and scratchy.

"Yeah. Do you want to see it?"

She didn't dare. "Maybe later." Maybe never, if she knew what was best for her.

He gestured in the opposite direction. "There're two baths and three other smaller rooms at the other end."

"What's in those other rooms?"

"Not much. One's my office, the other two have a few odds and ends, but no real furniture to speak of."

"Oh. So where am I staying?"

"Right this way." He crossed the hall and opened a door that led to another stairwell enclosed by narrow walls. "Be careful," he said over one shoulder as he began to climb the steps. "It's pretty steep."

Joanna made sure to concentrate on her footing, not Rio Madrid's finer points, as she scaled the stairs. She'd hate to have to explain that she'd taken a tumble while shamelessly staring at his butt.

At the top of the staircase, he opened another door and stepped inside the room. Joanna could only gape once she entered behind him. The whole area was swathed in sunlight spilling from the triple windows. The four-poster white canopy, covered in a frilly spread dotted with lilacs, the antique-white dresser, the immaculate hardwood floors with scattered throw rugs, looked like something from Victorian times. A matching lilac-colored chaise set below one window served as an invitation, a place to curl up with a good book and a cup of tea. Or with a lover on a lazy Sunday afternoon. She swallowed hard.

"Wow." It was all Joanna could manage at the moment. The room was almost twice as big as her old apartment, and no comparison as far as comfort was concerned. Never in her wildest imaginings had she envisioned this lovely place.

Rio laced his hands at his nape, his gorgeous face shining with satisfaction. "Yeah, it's nice. Not exactly my kind of decor, but I didn't have the heart to change anything. It has a personality all its own."

Joanna couldn't agree more. She walked to the bed and ran one hand down the post. "It's wonderful."

He pushed open another door and leaned against the wall next to it. "The bathroom's right here. It's not very big, and it only has a tub. An old claw-footed tub, but it's been restored. If you'd rather take a shower, you can use one of the second-floor bathrooms, or you could use mine. It's big."

Joanna locked on to his sensual smile. The image of showering with Rio Madrid arrived in great detail, including fogged-up glass from heavy breathing, not steam. Slick bodies, roving hands…

Good heavens. She didn't need to think about that now. Or ever. "Is there somewhere I can hang these?"

He pointed behind her. "In the closet."

She turned. "A closet? That's great. I haven't had one of those in a while." She hadn't had a lover in a while, either, a fact apparent every time Rio Madrid walked into the room.

After hanging her things in the moderate-size closet, she faced him again. "I guess I'll go get the rest of the boxes and bring them up."

"I'll do it in a minute. Care for some lunch?"

"Sure. I thought I'd go to the store and pick up a few groceries."

He pushed away from the wall. "I had my housekeeper do that yesterday."

"You have a housekeeper?"

"Yeah. I can't keep this place clean by myself, nor do I want to. She comes in twice a week, during the day."

"I think I've died and gone to heaven."

His grin resurfaced. "So your idea of heaven is a housekeeper?"

Joanna strolled to the bed and dropped onto the edge. "One of my ideas." Laughing, she fell back and sank into the soft mattress, arms raised above her head. "And this bed."

Rio slipped onto the bed beside her, thankfully not in a prone position. "I agree, a good feather bed qualifies as heavenly. So do other things."

She stared up at him. "What other things?" Had she really asked him such a leading question?

His smile faded into a seriously sensual expression. "Walking barefoot in grass. Swimming naked in a lake. Making love in the moonlight."

Joanna's heart lurched hard in her chest. She'd only done one of those things, but she hadn't walked barefoot in clover since she was a teenager. "Very poetic, Doctor."

"Not poetry, just perfection."

He was perfect, Joanna thought, from head to toe, at least superficially. But she knew soul deep that perfection was only an illusion. Everyone had flaws; Rio Madrid was no exception. But he also had an undeniable aura, a sensual magnetic field, drawing her in as if she were made of iron. She feared she might not be that strong if he made one move toward her.

Bolting from the bed, she stood before him, hands clasped tightly to keep from pulling the band out of his hair to let it completely fall just so she could experience its silky texture. "Okay, so what do you have in mind for lunch?"

The look he gave her said anything but food. His sexy smile had her thinking the same thing. "I'm kind of partial to peanut butter and jelly."

She returned his smile. "My son's favorite fare."

His features went solemn. "You know, Joanna, your son's welcome here. If you want to send for him, we could fix up one of the bedrooms."

Joanna experienced a twinge of emotion over his generosity. Few men would offer their homes to a single mom and her child. "I really appreciate that, but he's settled into school right now and I wouldn't want to uproot him again until I have a decent place of my own. Maybe that will happen by this summer."

Rio stood and sighed. "You've been here less than an hour and you're already thinking about leaving me."

Leaving *him?* "I can't stay here forever. But I appreciate this arrangement more than you know. It will give me a chance to get back on my feet financially." If he didn't pull the rug out from under her emotionally. Again, she didn't plan to let that happen. She'd done that once, let a man have her heart only to be left holding the remnants.

''We'll take it one day at a time,'' he said with confidence as he strolled toward the door. ''But in the meantime, let's go downstairs and grab some lunch. I'm starving.''

So was Joanna, for things she didn't dare want.

Four

"You have a fountain in your pool."

Rio couldn't stop the urge to tease Joanna a little. He had trouble stopping any urges where she was concerned. "A pool? No kidding? I didn't realize that. Guess I should go into the backyard more often."

Joanna glanced at him over one shoulder and smiled. "You are just full of it today, aren't you?"

Rio couldn't seem to get his fill of looking at her. He took the last bite of his sandwich and sat back in his chair, enjoying the view of Joanna staring out the breakfast nook's window. Her dark hair spiraled into curls between her shoulder blades. Natural curls, Rio suspected. She did things to jeans that shouldn't be allowed. She did things to him that would definitely be considered downright sinful.

Her slender hand rested against the pane, her nails short and neatly trimmed. Good, Rio thought. Long nails meant hard-to-hide scratches from lovemaking. And why the hell he believed that would happen between him and Joanna Blake would be anyone's guess. But something told him it could happen. Would happen. The carnal tension between them was gathering force, brewing like a spring storm, not that she would acknowledge it. At least not yet.

Pushing back from the table, Rio joined her at the window, standing close, but not too close. Patience would probably be the best way to handle what was happening between them, had been happening since New Year's Eve. Patience was something unfamiliar to him. He was the kind of guy who jumped in feetfirst and asked questions later when it came to his private life. Not a good idea in this instance.

Focusing on the backyard where Gabby lay gnawing a rawhide bone beneath an ancient cypress, he said, "There's a small hot tub in the corner of the pool with room for three."

"You, Gabby and your current girlfriend?" He heard a smile in her voice, and curiosity.

"Are you trying to get me to come clean about my personal life, Joanna?"

She turned, putting them in closer proximity yet maintaining an intangible distance. "It's really none of my business, but I imagine you've had a woman in your hot tub before."

He had, but not in a while. "I've been too busy to utilize my hot tub. Not today, though. Are you game?"

She frowned. "Are you nuts? It's forty degrees outside."

"That's why they call it a hot tub."

"It's also still daylight."

He propped one hand on the window beside her head,

leaned closer and lowered his voice. ‘‘Are you shy, Joanna Blake?’’

‘‘I’m a mother, for Pete’s sake.’’

‘‘And mothers are forbidden to use hot tubs?’’

‘‘Mothers don’t have the kind of figures most twenty-year-olds have. At least this mother doesn’t.’’

He allowed his gaze to slide down her body and linger in certain places. He wanted to do the same with his hands. ‘‘I seriously doubt that.’’

‘‘You’re seriously wrong.’’ A blush stained her fair cheeks. ‘‘Besides, I don’t own a decent swimsuit.’’

‘‘Who said anything about a swimsuit?’’

She turned back to the window. ‘‘What’s in that building over there?’’

Obviously she was more interested in continuing the tour than his suggestion. ‘‘It’s a pool house with an attached garage. I keep my bike in there.’’

‘‘Ten speed?’’

‘‘Harley.’’

Once more she faced him, this time hugging herself as if she needed protection from him. ‘‘You own a motorcycle and live in a mansion. I’d say you are a walking contradiction, Doctor.’’

He wished she’d call him by his first name. Right now he wasn’t the doctor. Right now he was a man in the company of a woman that he wanted too much. ‘‘Is that a problem?’’

‘‘Not really. It’s just that you’re not at all what I thought you’d be. At least at first.’’

‘‘And what was that?’’

‘‘An average male on the make. Your generous nature surprises me. So does your attraction to material things.’’

He took a step back, guilt dogging his steps as he made his way back to the table and reclaimed his seat.

"I've heard it all before, that old 'the love of money is the root of all evil' clause. But once you've been without it, money's not a bad thing to have. I imagine you know that."

"Yes, I do." Joanna joined him at the table and sat across from him with her blue eyes trained on his face. "I take it you didn't have much when you were growing up."

"I had next to nothing. My parents were migrant farmworkers, chasing the next job. After my father died, my mother moved from California to Texas. She worked as a fruit picker during the season and hired out as a domestic the rest of the time." And a midwife at night, something he didn't care to discuss.

"What happened to your father?"

Rio didn't like dredging up the past, but he'd left himself wide open to her questions. "An industrial accident involving some kind of machinery. I don't know many details."

"I'm sorry." She sounded as if she truly was.

"Don't be. I don't remember him. I was too young when it happened."

She rested her cheek on one palm. "So what made you decide to become a doctor?"

A long story, but he'd try for a condensed version. "My mother worked for a retired colonel. He knew I had an interest in medicine, so he took me under his wing since he didn't have any kids."

Joanna leaned forward. "Did he put you through medical school?"

That, and hell on earth. "Yeah, but first he put me into boarding school when I turned sixteen. I hated it. They made me cut my hair, robbed me of my heritage so I'd fit in. I've worn my hair long ever since."

"Your culture's very important to you, isn't it?"

"Some aspects, yes, some not." Especially those that defied logic.

"But you believe in your... What did you call it?"

"My onen. Mayan mythology. The sun god is a jaguar. It also foretells the arrival of foreigners."

"Foreigners?"

"Yeah. I think my mother chose that for me since I was born in the States. But she swore it came to her in a dream. I have a hard time believing it."

He'd never put much stock in dreams before he'd met Joanna Blake, before she had begun to disturb his own dreams. Surreal dreams. Sexual dreams.

Maybe his mother had been right to give him the onen. Joanna had come into his life, foreign to him, with a deeply engrained love for her child and a strong conviction in her work ethic. The consummate mother. A woman who deserved a considerate man to attend to her needs. Some of those needs Rio would have no problem tending, others he wasn't so sure.

Suddenly he wondered if this was the woman his mother had told him about, the stranger who would change his life for the better. A nice thing to consider, if he really believed in all that mystical stuff. Maybe he was just too jaded to believe in forever-after or love. He sure as hell didn't intend to settle down, conform to what society considered fitting—a marriage license and the average two kids.

Joanna remained silent with her elbows propped on the table, palms forming a resting place for her cheeks. She stared off into space as if she'd left him mentally, if not physically. He had a good idea where her thoughts had taken her.

"You're thinking about your son," he stated.

Joanna looked up, startled. ‘‘As a matter of fact, I was.’’

‘‘When was the last time you talked to him?’’

She straightened and fidgeted with a corner of the cloth place mat. ‘‘Two days ago, when I told my mom I was moving.’’

‘‘I bet it’s tough on him, being without you.’’

She smiled a sad mother’s smile. ‘‘It is. Tough on us both. But he’s a strong little boy. He’s had to be.’’

Rio wanted to know more about her, what made her tick. What made her sad other than the absence of her son. ‘‘Tough divorce?’’

‘‘In some ways, yes. Especially on Joseph, not that he had a great relationship with his father.’’

‘‘So his father’s totally out of the picture?’’

‘‘Very much so. I don’t even know where he is. Not that I want to know.’’

Sorry bastard. ‘‘Does Joseph ask about him?’’

‘‘Sometimes, but like you, he was too young to remember much about his dad. Joseph’s the best thing that came out of my marriage. He’s always been my strength.’’

The unshed tears glistening in Joanna’s blue eyes caused something deep inside Rio to hurt for her, made him want to take away that pain he saw all too clearly, even though she tried to hide it with a weak smile.

‘‘Call him now, Joanna.’’

She looked surprised and thankful. ‘‘Are you sure?’’

‘‘Yeah, I’m sure.’’

‘‘I’d like that. But I insist on paying you for the—’’

‘‘Forget it. Just call your son.’’ He nodded toward the phone hanging on the wall.

She quickly rose from the chair and strode to the phone. Rio thought he should probably leave, give her some privacy, but for some reason he stayed, maybe to provide some comfort if she needed it. He doubted she'd ask, though, or easily accept his consolation.

"Joseph, it's Mommy." Her face immediately brightened. "You're playing with your train? I'm so glad you like it, sweetie. I'm sorry I couldn't give you more Christmas presents, but maybe next year."

A long pause suspended the conversation until Joanna finally said, "I'll have to see about that bike. But you have to have training wheels until you learn to ride it."

Rio watched Joanna from the corner of his eye while he cleared the plates from the table. She twisted the cord round and round her finger, swiped at her face now and then, raised her chin and covered her mouth on occasion. He could tell she was trying hard not to cry. If only he could do something to rid her of those tears, at least temporarily. Get her mind off her troubles. Maybe he could.

After she hung up, he held out his hand to her. "Come here. I want to show you something."

She blinked then stared. "Where are we going?"

"It's a surprise."

"Surely you don't mean that hot tub."

"Nope. I want to show you my favorite place."

Joanna stared with wide-eyed wonder at a room that held every indoor form of recreation imaginable, including a freestanding basketball goal on one end. A pool table sat in the middle; electronic pinball games lined the paneled walls. The only thing that even hinted at adulthood was a bar that resembled something out of a saloon, complete with a mirrored background, shelves full of liquor and inverted glasses of every shape and size dangling from a row of holders above the counter.

"This used to be a formal dining room."

Rio's statement brought Joanna back into the real world, or his world, as the case may be. "It looks big enough to be a ballroom," she said.

"True. The room didn't have anything in it when I bought the house, so I turned the space into play town."

Play town was an accurate description, Joanna decided. Perfect, since it seemed Rio Madrid was still a little boy playing at being an adult—conservative doctor by day, adventurous adolescent by night. She'd known his kind before, been married to his kind, as a matter of fact. The kind of man that should be avoided at all costs.

But she couldn't avoid him at the moment since he was still holding her hand, looking as though he was awaiting approval on a job well done. Looking devastatingly handsome.

Tugging from his grasp, she walked to the leaf-scrolled wooden pool table, obviously expensive, maybe even an antique, more than likely five times more costly than her car.

She faced him and immediately noticed the pride in his expression. "Very interesting, Doctor. Is this what you do in your spare time when you're not in the hot tub?"

"Yeah. It helps me relax." He cocked one eyebrow. "Can I interest you in a game?"

Oh, yes. Oh, no! "What kind of game?"

He made a sweeping gesture around the room. "Take your pick, but I was thinking pool."

Now, this could be great fun, a chance for Joanna to play her own little game. "Oh, I don't know. It's been a long time. I've never been all that good." Not quite as good as her dad, but she could definitely hold her own.

"I'll go easy on you." His mellow, hypnotic voice made her think of slow and easy lovemaking. She suspected he would take his time, using his skilled hands, his mouth…

She should be horsewhipped for thinking such things, but Joanna couldn't deny that Rio Madrid was the kind of man that fantasies were made of. Nothing wrong with fantasies, she guessed, as long as she didn't allow them to take flight into reality.

Rio crouched at the end of the table, retrieved the balls from beneath and rolled them onto the felt surface. After he had them racked, he made his way to the cues hanging on the only bare space of wall. He grabbed two then came back to her. "Exactly how much experience do you have?"

A loaded question, especially since he posed it as if it had nothing to do with billiards. She took the pool stick he offered and a deep breath, but couldn't avoid brushing his hand, couldn't ignore the electric current that his touch generated throughout her whole body.

"As I've said, it's been a while." Been a while since she'd played pool, since she'd made love, since she'd even wanted to make love.

"I'll let you break then. Give you a head start."

She could use one at the moment, but she inherently knew it would take little time for Rio to catch up.

Determined to focus on the game, she rolled her shoulders to loosen up then walked to the end of the table, lined up the cue ball and studied the angle. Feigning ignorance, she asked, "Is this okay?"

"I'd say that."

Rio didn't appear to be looking at the ball, or the cue. He was looking straight at her cleavage, slightly exposed beneath her cotton blouse because of her position. Normally she would scold him. Normally she would button up to the neck and give him a dirty look. But she didn't feel all that normal. She felt wicked, delighting in the power she seemed to have over him at that moment.

About time. He'd mesmerized her on more than one occasion.

Finally he looked away and removed the rack. "It's all yours."

With a little thoughtful planning, Joanna managed to hit the cue ball exactly right, causing it to bounce twice but landing short of the other balls.

She straightened and tried to look contrite. "Sorry. Guess it's been longer than I thought."

"Maybe you're not holding the cue right." He took his time traveling to the other end of the table but didn't hesitate when he came up behind her and circled his arms around her, positioning her hand on the end of the stick. Joanna had all the confidence in the world on how to handle a cue, but she didn't have a clue on how to handle his nearness and still remain composed enough to play the game. He was warm against her back, hard, male, making her feel intoxicated as if she'd raided the old-timey bar and downed all the whiskey.

His breath fanned her face, fed the flame now spanning the length of her. He smelled like incense, spicy and exotic and tempting. Joanna continued to play ignorant, play at this game of chance where the stakes were high and losing all common sense could be the price she would pay if not careful.

"Now hold it steady," he said in a warm honeyed voice, thick and seductively sweet.

Steady? How could she? "I'll try."

The feel of him molded to her backside in all the right places had knocked her self-control for a loop, disturbed the timbre of her voice. She sounded like a mouse and felt like a woman. A woman in dire straits, enveloped in the solid arms of a man-boy with too much charm and the means to make her tremble, which she did, but only slightly.

With Rio's assistance—help she didn't really need—she broke the balls, effectively scattering them over the green felt surface, the way her composure scattered in his presence.

Much to her disappointment, and relief, he straightened and moved away.

His grin was confident, distracting. "You don't have to call the pocket right now since you're getting reacquainted with the game."

Joanna smiled to herself. Little did he know, the charade was now off and the competition on.

She leaned forward over the table, sensing Rio's scrutiny and trying hard to ignore it. If she didn't, she'd probably bounce the balls like ball bearings across the room with her first shot. "Twelve ball, corner pocket." After she said it, she did it. And again and again. With little effort, she cleared the table of all the striped balls.

Feeling sassy and satisfied, she said, "Well, Doctor, do you want to take a shot now before I take on the eight ball? I'll be glad to let you."

His smile looked sinister, and totally sexy. "You little sneak. Where'd you learn to play like that?"

"My dad."

"He taught you well."

"Yes, he did. As a matter of fact, he made a living at being a teacher. English teacher. So did my mom."

"Do you two still play?"

"He died when I was in college."

"I'm sorry."

''So am I, but he led a full life. I only wish he'd known his grandson.'' Joseph had been lacking a good male role model because of that fact, and his own father's apathy.

Rio laid his cue on the table, not bothering to take a shot. But he sure as heck was shooting holes in Joanna's resolve when he took the cue from her and laid it next to his then brushed his knuckles across her cheek. ''Best I can recall, none of my teachers were pool sharks. But then, I don't remember any of their daughters looking like you, either.''

Joanna forced herself away and strolled to the end of the room near the large picture window. She came upon a train set, intricately detailed down to the tiny pines and miniature houses. She bent and studied the tunnel opening from the foot of a tree-dotted hill. ''Joseph would love this. The train I gave him for Christmas is cheap plastic.''

She heard a *thwack* and glanced over her shoulder to find Rio dispensing the remainder of the balls into the pockets. His thermal shirt, pushed up at the sleeves, revealed his caramel skin threaded with masculine veins. His dark hair veiled his beautiful face when he leaned over, but it didn't matter. Joanna had practically memorized every detail.

He moved around the table and leaned over to make another shot. ''I used to watch one setup from the window at a train shop when I was a kid.'' He sent one ball into the pocket then straightened. ''I waited a lot of years to have one of my own.''

Joanna turned back to the train to keep from staring at him. When she heard footsteps behind her, she didn't dare turn around. ''Exactly how old are you, if you don't mind me asking?'' she said, aiming for something simple to say.

His hand came around her to push the control, setting the locomotive in motion along with her pulse. ''Literally? Thirty-three.''

She concentrated on the engine billowing steam, the multicolored cars as the train made the rounds on the track. ''And how old would you like to be?''

''That depends. When I'm in here, I'm thirteen again. In the outside world, I have to be the grown-up.''

''Well, I passed you up agewise last year.''

''You're only fourteen?'' he asked, mock seriously.

She turned and smiled at him. ''Ha, ha. Thirty-four. And a half.''

He inched a little closer, seeming to suck the air from the small space between them. ''An older woman. Intriguing. You look much younger. Not fourteen, but I would've guessed under thirty.''

''Sometimes I feel ancient.''

He stroked a hand over her cheek while studying her flushed face. ''You feel great.''

She was losing it, losing her will to resist him. Not a sensible thing to do, but rationality wasn't foremost on her mind at the moment. Rio was, with his penetrating eyes and a smile that certainly didn't belong on a boy. ''So you don't like being the grown-up?'' she asked.

''There's nothing wrong with being a man when the circumstance calls for it.''

He stopped the train now in mid-whistle, sending the room into silence. Then he pulled her flush against him and claimed her mouth with a kiss that could shake the tracks, the walls, shake Joanna into oblivion. It did. The gentle thrust of his tongue, the searing heat of his body, the strength of his steady hands as they traveled the length of her back then came to rest on her hips, acted on her like a magic charm, a spell she couldn't escape if her very life depended on it.

She draped her arms around his neck and sent her hands through his silky dark hair to explore. The kiss deepened, wild and needy, hungry and desperate. Desire advanced and her concerns retreated. Under Rio Madrid's expert guidance, she forgot to be afraid to want.

Rio was suddenly moving, taking her with him, leading her to who knew where. Perhaps a dreamland of his own making, like the mythical god he had spoken of, a sun god creating a firebrand with his mouth moving softly yet firmly against hers. She instinctively knew that he could take her places she'd never been before, if she allowed him.

He spun her around and backed her up without breaking the kiss. The edge of a table nudged her hip, the pool table, she decided, not that it mattered. The only thing that mattered was Rio and what he was doing to her body and her brain.

His lips drifted down the column of her throat, leaving a wet tingling path in their wake. His hand came to rest on the placket of her blouse, causing Joanna's heart to beat in a crazy cadence. He slipped the buttons with ease, allowing a cool draft of air to caress her heated skin. But the heat came back when his lips floated over the rise of her breasts.

Joanna laid her hands on his bent head, lost in the feel of his mouth on her skin, the deep, damp heat settling between her thighs.

He lifted his head and studied her with a potent golden gaze. ''*¿Me quiere usted?*''

She couldn't deny that she wanted him. She wanted this, wanted more, even though she shouldn't. ''Yes.''

"*Diga mi nombre.*" He made the demand in a low, persuasive voice.

She understood the Spanish, but not his request. "What?"

"Say my name."

Rio, her mind shouted, but she feared forming the word in her mouth. If she dispensed with the formality, he would no longer be the elusive doctor. If she continued to allow this heavenly assault on her senses, this prelude to pleasure, he could very well be her lover. And once more, she would be vulnerable to a man who wasn't what she needed at all.

But she did need this physical contact, to be desired as a woman. To satisfy cravings that had long been missing from her life. To forget herself in the arms of a man whose name meant "river." A man as seductive as dark waters, his lure a strong current promising to carry her away into uncharted territory.

She hesitated a moment longer, searching his eyes for a reason to stop. She saw only questions, then disappointment before he turned away from her.

Hands fisted at his sides, he muttered, "I promised myself I wouldn't do this."

Joanna clasped her shirt closed. "Do what?"

"Push you."

"You didn't push me. I let it happen."

He finally turned to her. "You're not ready."

She'd certainly felt ready. More than ready, and willing. "How can you say that?"

"Because you can't say my name. I'll be damned if I make love to a woman who calls me 'doctor.'"

Her gaping shirt forgotten, she braced her hands on her hips. "*Rio.* There, I said it. Are you happy now?"

His gaze went to her exposed bra and a half smile

curled the corners of his mouth. "Yeah, you said it, but not like you meant it."

He was driving her to distraction, making her insane. "I don't understand this at all."

"You understand it. You won't acknowledge it."

She redid her blouse with shaking fingers. "Forget it. This was a mistake anyway. All of it."

"Is it, *mi amante?*"

Her eyes snapped from the buttons to him. "I'm not your lover, remember?"

His smile disappeared, making way for a look that could dissolve the pool table behind her. "You will be, Joanna. When you're ready."

She hugged her arms to her middle. "You're mighty sure of yourself, aren't you?"

He folded his arms across his chest, his face an unreadable mask. "You can lie to yourself. You can pretend that nothing's going on between us. But I can't lie. I know how I feel when I'm holding you, and it's not just minor affection."

Why, oh, why hadn't she stayed home New Year's Eve? Stayed in her wretched apartment? She'd been comfortable with her existence, her celibacy, her choices. Why did *he* have to come along and disrupt her life? Why him, of all people—a man who made her ache, made her want, made her realize she possessed desires beyond all bounds?

The shrill of the phone startled Joanna and caused her to physically jump.

Rio grabbed up the cordless phone. "Dr. Madrid." He paced with his back to Joanna. After a time, he said, "Okay, I'm on my way."

He replaced his phone on the charger and turned. "I've got to go into the hospital."

Already she was missing him, and she hated that. "I thought you weren't on call."

"I'm not, but this is a special case. First baby. She's sixteen, scared. Her boyfriend didn't stick around. She wants me to deliver."

Her admiration for him increased more than she thought possible. "I guess she needs you."

"Yeah. Nice to know someone does now and then." He sounded almost sad, as alone as Joanna felt much of the time.

He stopped in the doorway. "Make yourself at home. There's a casserole in the fridge you can heat up for dinner. My housekeeper left it for me."

"I'll make do." She needed to say something, but she wasn't sure what. "Rio?" The word rolled easily off her tongue.

His smile appeared, slowly. A satisfied smile. "Yeah?"

"Since this is a first baby, you might be a while, so I just wanted to say good-night and thanks for everything. I hope you get some sleep."

He braced one hip against the door frame and released a mirthless laugh. "Sleep? Not in a million years."

Five

Joanna couldn't sleep. Maybe it was the strange house, the strange bed, the knowledge that she was all alone again.

Since retiring for the night, she had listened carefully for the sound of Rio's return but hadn't heard a thing, even from Gabby who was still outside, as far as she knew. Of course, Gabby didn't strike her as being much of a watchdog.

Joanna had gone to her room following a meager dinner of tuna casserole and an hour spent watching some inane sitcom. Now she sat in bed and tried to read materials to prepare for a continuing-education course she was due to take in the spring. She quickly abandoned that for a glitzy magazine heralding the breakups of rich and indulgent celebrities. Tiring of that, she tossed the magazine aside and stared at the ceiling.

Maybe if she took another shower, she might relax.

A hot bath… The hot tub? Well, that was an option. Since Rio was gone, she could hide away in there without notice. But what if he came home? Gabby would warn her, hopefully giving her enough time to sneak back inside.

Joanna rose from the bed and rummaged in the dresser for the only swimsuit she owned. It was black, basic, the only thing daring about it came in the form of sheer netting that covered the midriff but revealed little more than a hint of flesh.

After donning the suit, she retrieved an oversize towel from the linen closet and padded down the stairs. Just to be on the safe side, she tiptoed to Rio's room. The door was partially open and it creaked when she gave it a push. Her heart jumped, but thankfully she found the king-size bed still made, its owner absent. She took a chance and snapped on the light for a better look.

The bedroom was without embellishments, masculine, from the heavy pine bed covered in a black and gold spread to the posh tan carpeting. Several artifacts were set out on the tables in a small sitting area to her right, clay pots of every shape and size, a few polished stones, some small sculptures. On the wall over the black marble fireplace's mantel hung an odd-looking calendar sporting a moon, stars and the sun. Yet the enticing scent exclusive to Rio appealed to her most of all.

Feeling nervous over invading his privacy, Joanna retreated out of the room and started down the stairs and into the backyard. The night was moonless, cold, and she almost reconsidered, but she'd already come this far, no use turning back now. After her eyes adjusted to the limited light, she headed for the hot tub, pulling up short a few feet away when she caught sight of the dark, imposing figure cast in shadows spilling across the water's surface.

Rio.

Joanna saw a chance at escape until Gabby whined from her perch on the ground near the steps that led to the tub.

"Looks like you and I had the same idea."

His deep voice stopped Joanna's departure, nearly stopped her heart. "I couldn't sleep, so I thought this might help me relax." She was anything but relaxed at the moment. "But since you're—"

"There's plenty of room for us both."

Even if the tub spanned the length of the yard, she doubted there would be enough room for her and Rio Madrid, together. Not if she wanted to keep her guard up, her head on straight and her clothes on.

"Join me," he said in a seductive voice that promised untold pleasure. "The water's great."

The water wasn't her main concern at the moment. Rio's unexpected presence was. Did she dare join him? She was afraid to move forward, afraid to move at all.

She could do this, act like an adult, not some flighty, smitten teenager. Stay for a little while. Only a little while.

Clasping the towel to her chest, she moved on sluggish legs. She managed the steps but couldn't manage to take her eyes off him once she reached the top. The darkness didn't allow her to make out much more than his shadowy form. Probably a good thing since she noted that his clothes were piled on the bench in the corner. All of them, she suspected.

Keeping the towel close to her body, she sat on the ledge opposite him and dangled her feet in the water. "Wow. This is much hotter than I realized."

She saw a flash of white teeth. "The temperature just rose a few degrees, among other things."

Don't look, Joanna. But she did, and luckily she couldn't see anything much, not that she didn't really want to.

Then he reached behind him and snapped on the light. The jets whirred to life, setting a foaming mound of bubbles into action, along with Joanna's pulse.

She looked away, afraid she might see something she didn't need to see, namely all of Rio's body now reclined in one corner of the tub. Every fine detail.

"Are you going to get in, Joanna, or just sit there until you turn into an ice cube?"

She ventured a look in Rio's direction. His hands were stacked behind his head, his hair wet and much too sexy for words. She chafed her palms down her arms. "It is kind of chilly." Chills that were a direct result of viewing his bare chest, his sultry smile.

"It's warm enough in here." He gave her a lingering assessment. "Nice suit."

She looked down, then back up again. "It's all I have."

"I mean it, Joanna. It looks great on you."

Searching for a switch of subjects, she asked, "How did the birth go?"

"Without a hitch. In fact she delivered in two hours. A healthy baby girl. A little underweight, but okay."

"Then you've been in the hot tub all this time?"

A deep chuckle rumbled in his chest. "Now if that were true, I'd be shriveled up like a prune. Believe me, I'm not."

Again she wanted to look below the water's depths, find a break in the bubbles, find his tattoo and the territory beneath. But she forced her eyes to remain on his face. "How long have you been home?"

He dropped his arms and stroked one hand across his chest. Joanna couldn't help but imagine her own hand there. "Long enough to take a quick swim then get in here. I stayed at the hospital until she said goodbye to her daughter."

"Said goodbye?"

"She's putting the baby up for adoption."

Joanna's heart began to ache with that knowledge. Being without Joseph for the past few months had been devastating, and only a temporary situation. She couldn't begin to imagine how heartbreaking it would be to give up a child permanently. "I'm sure that was a difficult decision," she said with a sigh.

"Yeah, but for the best. She wants to continue with school. She doesn't have any money since her parents kicked her out, but she's got a relative willing to take her in, as long as it's only her and not a child."

"I hope they find a nice family for the baby."

"I hope so, too. It's tough not being wanted."

How odd that he would say such a thing since he'd spoken so fondly of his mother. How strange that he sounded so sad. "I wouldn't know." At least not from a parental standpoint. On the other hand, she knew quite well how it felt not to be wanted by a husband. "Sounds like you might have had some experience with that."

His sudden slight shift was the only thing that indicated his discomfort. "Oh, my mother wanted me, all right, until she married my stepfather."

"You never mentioned him before."

"I did. The colonel."

"The man your mother worked for?"

"Yeah. And after they married, they sent me away to

boarding school. Expected me to conform, be what they wanted me to be, in his case, white. It wouldn't do for a decorated military man to have a poor multiracial brat running around, now, would it?"

The venom in his tone caused Joanna to flinch. "But his last name was Madrid."

"No. It was Burlington. He adopted me, but I used my own father's name in med school. I had it legally changed back after the colonel's estate was settled."

"I'm sorry that you had to live like that."

"Well, at least I got all this in the deal." He made a sweeping gesture around the area. "He left all his money to me, his ranch, which I sold the first chance I got. I didn't want to hang on to those memories."

Again he had thrown her off balance with his revelations. He was more an enigma now than ever.

The strap on Joanna's swimsuit slipped off her shoulder. When she started to push it up, he said, "Leave it."

For some reason she did, even though the falling strap pulled the neckline of the suit lower, exposing the top of her breast.

"Get in, Joanna," he commanded in a deep, drugging voice. "I won't bite. Much." He topped off the request with a wicked grin.

Joanna suspected it would take more energy than she owned to resist his pull. But she didn't have the desire to fight him any longer, at least at the moment. She could do this, keep her distance, remain focused and maintain a firm grip on reality.

Tossing her towel aside, she slipped into the welcoming water across from Rio. Her fair skin was cloaked in a translucent blue because of the tinted light. But Rio was dark and dangerous, the proverbial calm before the storm.

Tipping her head back, Joanna closed her eyes and tried to block out Rio's image.

A hand caught her wrist, prompting her eyes to snap open and her pulse to quicken. Slowly he pulled her forward then turned her until she came to rest between his thighs, her back to his chest.

"Relax," he whispered. "I'm not going to hurt you."

Oh, but he could, and quite sufficiently, at least from an emotional perspective. She couldn't think about that now, or worry about it, because her attention was drawn to something against her lower back. She didn't have to guess what that *something* was.

He rested his lips against her bare shoulder then worked his way up her neck. She shuddered at the sensations, trembled when he slipped the other strap down. He streaked his knuckles back and forth over the rise of her breasts. She wanted him to keep going, ached for him to keep going, but he didn't.

"Take it off," he murmured. "You'll feel better."

Abandoning good sense, Joanna slipped her arms out of the straps and tugged the bodice down, baring her breasts completely to his eyes, his hands. Yet he still didn't touch her, at least not intimately.

He did wrap his arms around her shoulders, his hands clasped together above her breasts. Joanna marveled at the contrasting colors of their skin—hers almost alabaster white, his the color of warm chocolate. Marveled at her sudden lack of inhibition, her indescribable need for his touch.

Her legs floated upward and so, it seemed, did her whole being. She waited for Rio to remove her suit completely but when he didn't, she worked it down and away and watched as it twisted into the current.

"Now that's more like it," he said. "Don't you feel a sense of freedom?"

She did, and she also felt light-headed, uncontrolled and needy.

She looked back at him. His golden earring twinkled, his eyes a near match in color. His strong, sharp features delineated by the glow of the light bouncing from the water's surface mesmerized her, as did his lips outlined by the shadow of evening whiskers playing over his jaw.

He watched her for a long moment, waited for something but she wasn't sure what. He made no move to touch her intimately yet his eyes never left hers.

Unable to stand the suspense any longer, she palmed his jaw and brought his mouth to hers. He kissed her deeply, deliberately, with a steady glide of his tongue in a slow, seductive foray, back and forth until she lost all sense of time or place or purpose. A slight moan climbed up her throat and she tried to stop its progress. Honestly she did, but she couldn't. She also couldn't halt the cravings, the way he held her prisoner with his capable mouth. She felt the glide of his erection against her back as he pulled her closer to him, his hips lifting on the current. It was the most erotic moment she had ever experienced, knowing how close she was to giving him everything, finally acknowledging a sensual facet of herself that she had long ago learned to deny.

Yet when his hand drifted to her breast, Joanna tensed, a knee-jerk reaction she couldn't control.

He broke the kiss and rubbed his thumb over her lip. "Do you want this, Joanna?"

She tucked her head beneath his chin, turning her face into his neck, away from his questioning gaze. "Yes."

She sensed he would treat her with consideration and care, with skill. And he did, with a light stroke on one nipple, then the other. She melted against him and closed her eyes, immersed herself in his touch, the ripples of water flowing over her.

The night wrapped around her like a comforting mantle, as comforting as Rio's embrace, his sleek touch. Something inside Joanna broke away. Her caution, her concerns. All that mattered was him, the feelings he stirred within her, the undeniable passion, the yearning that was so foreign yet so welcome.

As if she'd totally detached herself from the lonely, celibate shell her life had been to this point, she laid her palm on his hand and guided it downward. He paused at her belly immediately below her navel, brushing his knuckles back and forth in a slow, torturous rhythm.

"Tell me what you want, Joanna," he whispered.

She didn't want to think, or to consider what was about to happen. She wanted him, only him, and to be the woman that he desired. "Touch me."

He sifted his fingertips through the tangle of curls between her thighs, then on to her susceptible flesh with a gentle yet unyielding caress. "Like this?"

"Yes." The word hissed out on the wings of a broken breath.

His murmured sensual words danced around in her head as the bubbles danced over her body. His fingertip made gentle passes over places too long ignored then slipped deep inside her, slowly, deliberately.

The steam rose around her as Rio's touch swathed her in a heavy fog of desire. The pressure began to mount beneath his insistent strokes. So did the need to resist for fear of completely losing herself. But no matter how hard she tried to fight it, prolong its arrival, the climax came with the force of a tempest, sucking her breath from her lungs, her thoughts from her brain. Her pulse throbbed in her ears, her body trembled. She felt weak, boneless, satisfied.

Rio held her through the aftermath for a time, still toying with the curls with gentle fingers. She wanted to tell him to touch her again, and again. She wanted to take him inside her, all of him, to know what it felt like to be totally consumed by a man who held such sensual power over her.

"Are you okay?" he whispered.

Was she *okay?* She was more than okay. More than ready to continue. She could only nod, her cheek rubbing against the warm damp skin at his neck.

"Good. Maybe now you'll sleep."

With that, he tipped her face up, brushed a kiss over her lips then worked his way from behind her. "Stay as long as you'd like."

When he left the tub, Joanna could only stare at him, stare at his sculpted buttocks, his damp hair resting on his shoulders, his strong spine glistening with moisture. And when he turned, the evidence that he was still aroused definitely caught her attention before he slipped on his jeans without bothering to dry off.

Joanna felt self-conscious, alone and naked, cold and confused. She crossed one arm over her breasts and searched beneath the water's surface for her suit. Not finding it, she hoisted herself out of the tub and grabbed for the towel to secure it around her.

"Where are you going?" she asked through chattering teeth as she sat on the bench near the tub, unable to stand any longer.

"To bed."

"But...I...you..." She sounded like a stammering idiot, a desperate woman.

"I what?"

"I thought maybe we might finish this."

He slipped his shirt over his head. "Not tonight, Joanna. This was for you." He knelt and fished her suit from the water, squeezed it out, then tossed it at her. It hit the wooden deck at her feet with a soggy thump.

She snatched up the suit and stood, fighting to control her anger. "Oh, so you were doing me a favor, were you? Poor desperate Joanna Blake who hasn't been with a man in years."

He inclined his head. "You haven't?"

Nothing like giving herself away. "No, I haven't, and I don't need your favors." She shot a pointed look below his belt. "So is this some kind of test of your strength, or do you plan to take care of that yourself?"

He ate up the space between them in two long strides, clasped her hand and pressed her palm against his erection. "I plan for you to take care of this but only when you're ready."

He took a step back and Joanna rolled her eyes to the night sky. "We're back to that again? I did what you wanted. I said your name, several times. What do I have to do next, recite poetry?"

"You have to learn to trust me. You have to believe that I'm worthy enough to make love to you in every way."

"And I have no say in the matter? We'll make love when *you* say the time's right?"

"We'll make love when you come to me without my coercion. And not a minute before."

He clicked off the jets and lights in the tub then turned and sprinted down the steps with Gabby following at his heels. The sound of the back door closing jarred Joanna out of her shock. Suddenly she felt to-the-marrow cold, and alone.

She also felt determined. If Rio Madrid wanted to play games, then bully for him. She didn't have to play along. If he was waiting for her to come to him, then he definitely had another think coming.

She didn't need him, and that's what she kept telling herself all through the night.

Two long, restless nights, Joanna thought as she readied for her next patient the following Monday afternoon. One equally chaotic day. When she turned on the water in the exam room's stainless sink, a flashback assailed her—blue lights, skilled hands, naked flesh, absolute paradise.

She fumbled with the blood pressure cuff, dropped the chart and knocked her coffee cup over onto the counter. Luckily it flipped sideways into the sink, saving the carpet from a good dousing, saving Joanna from a fit of oaths directed at Rio Madrid.

She definitely had the good doctor to thank for her distraction as well as the heat flowing through her body on a stream of remembrance. She needed to stop thinking about what had happened Saturday night, as well as what hadn't happened. So far, that's about all she'd thought of since the moment she'd awakened at dawn, alone.

Joanna supposed she should be thankful Rio hadn't changed his mind and come to her. But she wasn't. As unwise as it seemed, she would have welcomed him into her bed, into her body without a second thought, but probably not without regret.

Yes, she should be very thankful he'd stayed away, avoided her yesterday as well. Instead, she was frustrated and needy and still wanted him as much as she had two nights before. As much as she had that first night when he'd kissed her.

"Knock, knock," Allison Cartwright called from the open door. "Do you have a few minutes?"

Joanna pulled a few paper towels from the metal dispenser and wiped the water from her hands, wishing she could as easily wipe Rio from her mind. "Come on in. My next patient's not due in for another ten minutes or so. What's up?"

Allison strode into the exam room, her auburn hair swinging back and forth where it fell over her shoulders. After dropping her small frame into the nearby chair, she let out a strained breath and stretched out her long legs. "My feet are starting to swell and my hips are expanding to dangerous proportions. I have to pee every fifteen minutes because I think junior here is sitting on my bladder. But that's okay because in about six weeks, he'll be here and I'll forgive him everything."

Joanna grinned. "Are you still convinced it's a boy?"

Allison gave her round belly a pat. "You betcha. He's so active that I can't help but believe he's training for soccer."

"You could always find out during an ultrasound."

"Nope. I want to be surprised."

"By the way, have you seen Dr. Madrid lately?"

"Actually, that's what I wanted to talk to you about. Dr. Madrid."

Joanna tried not to push the internal panic button yet she couldn't help but worry that maybe people already knew about her recent living arrangements. Ludicrous. Allison had no way of knowing since she worked across town for a prominent law firm. Unless Rio had told her. Surely not. "What about Dr. Madrid?"

"I've come to the decision that I'm going to use the

center, as long as you'll attend my birth. I'm just not sure how I'm going to tell him. He's been so good to me, and he's such a great doctor, but I really don't want to have my baby in the hospital.''

Joanna crossed the room and leaned back against the exam table, facing Allison. ''Are you absolutely sure? You've told me that you were considering an epidural, and you know we don't provide that here.''

''I'm sure. And I'm no longer worried about the pain aspect because I know you'll be with me through the whole thing. To be honest, there are other reasons why I don't want to have this baby at Memorial.''

Joanna frowned. ''You're not obligated to tell me, but does this have something to do with the baby's father?''

Allison's gaze faltered. ''You could say that, but I'd rather not say anything more.''

''I understand.'' Obviously the father worked at the hospital. Joanna briefly wondered if maybe he was married. Such a shame if that were true, but she had a hard time believing Allison would fall into that trap. However, Joanna knew all too well how persuasive men could be, as well as deceptive. ''Would you like me to tell Dr. Madrid about your decision?''

Allison frowned. ''In all fairness, I need to tell him myself, but if you could just sort of pave the way so he won't be quite as shocked.''

''No problem,'' she said, although she didn't exactly relish the idea. ''I'll mention it to him tonight.''

''Tonight?''

Oh, heavens, how was she going to get out of this one? ''Uh, well, yes. If I see him tonight. For some reason. That's possible, if there's some reason for seeing him.'' *Wow, Joanna. That sounded really coherent.*

Allison sent her a knowing smile. ''I think the midwife doth protest too much.'' She leaned forward and lowered her voice. ''Is he as good as he looks?''

Right on cue, heat rushed from Joanna's neck to her scalp. ''I wouldn't know.'' Not that she didn't want to know. Actually she did know on a limited basis.

''Are you sure?''

She was sure about one thing—she needed to end this conversation now. After a quick glance at the clock, Joanna said, ''Oh, look. It's time for my next patient.''

Allison rose from the chair with a grace Joanna had always longed for and started toward the door. ''Okay, Nurse Blake, I'm not going to bug you since we're all entitled to our little secrets.'' She circled her slender fingers around the doorknob and turned to Joanna with a wily grin. ''But as soon as you find out how good the doctor really is, be sure to let me in on it.''

With that she breezed out the door, and Joanna resisted the urge to throw water on her face to cool the sudden heat.

Water. Soothing warm water, bubbles twirling over her body, gentle fingers dancing over tender flesh…

Joanna slapped her palms to her cheeks as if she could jar the memories from her mind.

Darn Rio Madrid. When she did see him again, she would make it a point to mention Allison Cartwright. And she'd make it quite clear that the game was up, she didn't want to play, so he'd best keep his distance.

Now if she only remembered to keep hers.

Six

After two lengthy deliveries, Rio arrived home early Friday morning slightly before dawn. He built a fire in the den, stripped off his shirt and collapsed onto the sofa with Gabby.

Since Joanna had moved in with him two weeks ago, he'd barely seen her due to their conflicting schedules, at least not as much as he'd wanted. They had shared dinner a few nights, and he did have to admit that he'd greatly enjoyed the meals she'd prepared, their casual conversations, and definitely the way she always made him smile with some amusing story about her son. He appreciated the fact that she really listened to him when he'd had a particularly tough day, appreciated their shared concern for their patients. Yet he'd sensed the discomfort those times when—unable to resist—he'd done nothing more than reach out and touch her face or her hand.

The Silhouette Reader Service™ — Here's how it works:

Accepting your 2 free books and mystery gift places you under no obligation to buy anything. You may keep the books and gift and return the shipping statement marked "cancel." If you do not cancel, about a month later we'll send you 6 additional books and bill you just $3.57 each in the U.S., or $4.24 each in Canada, plus 25¢ shipping & handling per book and applicable taxes if any.* That's the complete price and — compared to cover prices of $4.25 each in the U.S. and $4.99 each in Canada — it's quite a bargain! You may cancel at any time, but if you choose to continue, every month we'll send you 6 more books, which you may either purchase at the discount price or return to us and cancel your subscription.

*Terms and prices subject to change without notice. Sales tax applicable in N.Y. Canadian residents will be charged applicable provincial taxes and GST. Credit or Debit balances in a customer's account(s) may be offset by any other outstanding balance owed by or to the customer.

If offer card is missing write to: Silhouette Reader Service, 3010 Walden Ave., P.O. Box 1867, Buffalo NY 14240-1867

BUSINESS REPLY MAIL

FIRST-CLASS MAIL PERMIT NO. 717-003 BUFFALO, NY

POSTAGE WILL BE PAID BY ADDRESSEE

SILHOUETTE READER SERVICE
3010 WALDEN AVE
PO BOX 1867
BUFFALO NY 14240-9952

She should consider herself lucky, Rio decided. He'd wanted to touch her elsewhere, kiss her everywhere. He'd fought to keep his hands to himself, battled to keep from coming up behind her while she'd stood at the stove cooking, wanting badly to turn up the heat by slipping his hand inside the baggy sweatpants she tended to wear after business hours, to make her react the way she had in the hot tub. But he'd decided to stick to his guns and wait for her to make the next move, even if it was killing him to do so.

Thoughts of making love to her—really making love to her—made him brick hard, made him want to groan with frustration. He lowered his fly an inch to provide some relief, but it didn't help all that much. Only one thing would alleviate the problem, and she was upstairs, fast asleep.

After yanking the band from his hair, Rio tipped his head back against the leather sofa and propped his feet on the coffee table. With Gabby curled up next to him, he flipped on the TV with the remote and settled for some infomercial hawking a miracle cleaner. Normally he would try to find something more entertaining, or at least something that might put him to sleep, at least for an hour or so before he had to return to the hospital to make his morning rounds.

Right now his thoughts centered on Joanna, on the fact that she was upstairs in bed, alone, and he was on the couch, hurting like hell from wanting her. From wanting to touch her again, only this time with his mouth as well as his hands. From needing to be inside her with an urgency as unfamiliar as having a woman living with him. A woman he wanted way too much.

But he'd been dead serious when he'd told her that he wasn't going to make love to her until she came to him. It needed to be a conscious decision, not duress, that brought her to his bed. She had to make up her mind that she was willing to enter into a relationship that might never be more than two people enjoying intimacy.

He wished he could offer her more, but he wasn't sure he could. An integral part of him feared the loss of freedom since he'd given up so many liberties in his lifetime. But more important, he wasn't certain he was cut out for marriage or fatherhood; his own example had been anything but satisfactory.

At times he had considered settling into that role, yet he'd never found a woman who'd encouraged the kind of feelings that led to a serious commitment.

Except for the woman upstairs. Maybe that's why having Joanna Blake in his life was beginning to scare the hell out of him. And as bad as he hated to admit it, his burgeoning feelings for her did alarm him on a very distinct level. He'd mistakenly thought he could handle it. Handle having her here yet not having her completely. He didn't like his weakness, nor did he want to act on his desire unless he knew for certain she was willing to accept the terms. But he wasn't sure how long he could remain strong in her presence—emotionally and physically.

Gabby whined, cocked her head to one side and stared at the doorway from the entry. Rio looked over his shoulder to see Joanna's form cast in a mix of gold and silver light coming from the TV and the fire. She trudged into the room wearing a thigh-length flannel nightshirt and a pair of baggy socks, her hair a tangle of curls. She was a mess, and Rio couldn't remember ever wanting someone as much as he wanted her at that moment.

His body had begun to calm a few moments before only to be brought back to life by her sudden appearance. If he were any kind of gentleman, he'd grab a throw pillow and shove it on his lap to hide his current predicament. But from the looks of Joanna's sleepy expression, he doubted she'd notice.

After Joanna settled into the oversize club chair catty-corner from the couch, he asked, "What are you doing up so early?"

When he unconsciously rubbed a hand over his bare chest, her gaze followed the movement, continuing to his abdomen and lower, where his jeans were partially undone, serving to make him even more uncomfortable.

"What are you doing...up?" She jerked her gaze back to the television.

Rio almost laughed—a pain-filled, joyless laugh. Instead, he laced his hands behind his head and released a slow, even breath in an effort to conceal his uneasiness. "I haven't been to bed yet. In fact, I just got home. Busy night so I'm still high on adrenaline." High on her. High on the prospect of peeling her faded flannel nightshirt slowly off her body and making long, hard love to her in front of the fire. The flame had dwindled due to his halfhearted attempts, but the blaze burning below Rio's belt generated enough heat to fuel the entire city.

Joanna stretched and yawned. "I couldn't sleep any longer. Too much on my mind, I guess."

She sounded slightly distressed, and Rio's concern for Joanna helped to pacify his cravings somewhat. "Is work not going well?"

She shook her head. "Work is fine. I got a letter from my mom and Joseph yesterday."

His concern increased. "Something wrong?"

"Not really. Joseph is doing well in school, making A's although he's had a little trouble with talking in class." She smiled. "He gets that from his father."

Rio dropped his feet from the table and leaned forward, arms draped on his thighs. ''You're missing your son,'' he said in a simple statement of fact.

''I miss him every night, every day, especially when it's cold. It reminds me of when he was born, in November. The day I took him home, it was around thirty degrees, crisp and clear outside. I spent that first day holding him. He was so tiny and I was so scared. Just the thought of molding someone's life is overwhelming. But I like to think about that particular day when it was just us, getting to know each other.''

''What about your husband?''

Joanna hugged her knees to her chest, her feet balanced on the edge of the chair as she turned her attention to the smoldering logs. ''Oh, he was out celebrating the fact that he had a son. He started celebrating the day I went into labor and didn't quit for about a week.''

''But he was with you during the birth.''

''Well, no. Adam wasn't very good at that sort of thing. But I was lucky, only four hours of labor.''

''You were lucky where the labor was concerned. I can't say the same for your choice in husbands.''

Joanna nailed him with blue eyes that looked almost translucent in the muted light. ''He was very charming, a big talker.'' She nodded toward the TV and the hyperactive host extolling the virtues of the cleaner in a booming voice. ''Just like that guy. The pitch sounds great and then you soon discover you've purchased a faulty product. I've learned that when it sounds too good to be true, most likely it is.''

God, Rio despised her ex more and more with each revelation and he didn't even know the guy. But he did know that Joanna had told the truth, and that was enough justification for his hatred. ‘‘Did the bastard ever give you what you needed?’’

Her gaze snapped to his. ‘‘He gave me Joseph.’’

‘‘He should be supporting you financially.’’

‘‘With what? His looks?’’ Her tone bore the anger of a woman scorned, and rightfully so. ‘‘He couldn’t keep a job while I was in school. I doubt he has one now.’’

‘‘You were in school when the baby was born?’’

‘‘Medical school. Second year. That’s how we ended up in San Antonio.’’

The disclosure threw Rio mentally off-kilter. ‘‘Medical school?’’

She tucked her legs beneath her and folded her arms across her breasts. ‘‘Yeah. I didn’t exactly plan to have a baby then. I wanted to wait until I finished but…’’ Her gaze faltered. ‘‘I foolishly thought that having a child might settle Adam down. Obviously I was mistaken.’’

‘‘Obviously. But you don’t regret having Joseph.’’

‘‘No. He’s my whole life.’’

Rio saw undeniable love reflecting from her beautiful blue eyes. A mother’s love. And he realized now, more than ever, she did merit a man who could love her the way she deserved to be loved.

‘‘I had no idea you planned to be a doctor,’’ he said, ill at ease over his sudden feelings of inadequacy where Joanna was concerned, with how little emotionally he had to offer.

‘‘There are quite a few things you don’t know about me.’’

He knew that he respected her, that he admired her selfless love for her child. That he hated what her husband had done to her. That he wished he had more to give. ‘‘I’d like to know more about you, Joanna,’’ he found himself saying with sincerity. He did want to know her, and he was only beginning to scratch the surface.

A reluctant grin curled the corners of her full lips. ‘‘I think we’ve skipped a few important steps, considering you now know what I look like naked.’’

She could have gone all day without saying that. His uncooperative body could have gone all year without hearing it.

Shifting from the building tension in his groin, he opted to revisit something they’d discussed the day she’d moved into his house in an attempt to quell the urge to carry her to his bed. ‘‘The offer still stands about having Joseph come to live here. Then he could be with you every day.’’

She sighed. ‘‘I really appreciate it, but as I’ve said before, he needs to stay in school throughout the remainder of the year now that he’s settled.’’

‘‘Okay, but if you change your mind, you know he’s welcome.’’

To his surprise, she scooted out of the chair, walked to the sofa and hovered above him. ‘‘Are you planning to go to bed any time soon?’’

He wanted to go to bed with her, but not unless she extended the invitation. ‘‘In a while.’’

She looked at him expectantly before her gaze traveled to his mouth. ‘‘Guess you’re really tired, huh?’’

Not so tired that if she asked, he’d make love to her until the sun rose in a couple of hours. But only if she asked. ‘‘Is there something you need from me?’’

A long silence ensued as she stood there opening and closing her fists and biting her lower lip. It took a major effort on Rio’s part not to take her hands, pull her into his lap—straddling his lap—so he could feel her against him, let her know that he needed to be inside her more than he needed sleep. For a brief moment he thought she might actually come to him and soothe the ache building to an unbearable intensity below his tattered jeans.

The moment ended when her gaze shifted away. ‘‘Actually, there’s something I need to tell you. In fact, I’ve been meaning to tell you for a while now.’’

Her serious tone indicated seduction was the last thing on her mind. Or maybe he’d only imagined the longing reflecting in her blue eyes. He patted the cushion next to him in hopes that she might reconsider. ‘‘Have a seat.’’

She stared at the sofa as if it were covered in spikes, not leather. ‘‘It can wait. You need your rest.’’

Aside from needing her in a very fundamental way, he needed to know what was bugging her. ‘‘A few more minutes aren’t going to matter.’’

Finally, she claimed a seat on the far end of the couch as if he were contagious. ‘‘It’s about Allison Cartwright. I believe she’s decided to use the center for the birth.’’

Rio wasn’t exactly surprised, nor was he exactly thrilled. Yet he had to accept Allison’s decision, even if he didn’t like it. ‘‘I understand why she feels she has to do it.’’

‘‘But you’re angry about it.’’

‘‘Not angry. Concerned.’’

Joanna moved closer, once again jump-starting his awareness of her—the way she smelled, the way he knew she would feel beneath him. ‘‘Rio, I promise she’ll be fine. The pregnancy is going very well, right?’’

‘‘Right.’’ He couldn’t disregard his apprehension any more than he could disregard his desire for Joanna Blake. He centered his gaze back on the TV, away from her assessment. ‘‘But anything could happen.’’

"Or nothing could happen aside from the birth of a healthy baby. You and I both know that."

He could feel her staring at him, dissecting him. Right now he was just too damn tired to discuss this. Wound too tight to think about anything other than escaping before he released all his frustration by taking Joanna into his arms to try a little sensual persuasion. "Just promise me that if something does come up, you'll bring her to the hospital."

"I'll call you if something happens, but I seriously doubt it will."

"Fine." He came to his feet only then realizing the extent of his exhaustion. He might as well be wearing concrete shoes, he decided as he headed toward the kitchen. At least his body had calmed somewhat.

"Rio."

Joanna's smooth, soothing voice turned him around, teased his libido awake again. "Yeah."

"You know, you could still be present for the birth if you'd like."

"No, thanks."

She frowned. "I hope one day you'll trust me enough to tell me what happened that made you so opposed to nonhospital births."

"Nothing happened." Except he'd watched a young woman die when he was barely old enough to watch that same woman give birth. "Just consider me overly cautious."

"Are you going to your room?"

Not such an appealing thought without her accompanying him. "I'm going to grab the paper and have some coffee first."

"Then I need to ask a favor."

He could think of several favors he'd like to provide for her, even dead tired. "Shoot."

"Do you mind if I use your shower? I won't take long."

"No problem." It was a problem, at least for Rio. Knowing Joanna was in his shower—naked and wet—would prevent him from sleeping at all should he decide to grab a quick nap in his bedroom. But that wouldn't keep him from honoring her request. In fact, he was beginning to think he might have a damn hard time refusing her anything.

She wasn't alone.

Through the mist clinging to the transparent shower door, Joanna saw Rio leaning against the bathroom entry, his arms folded over his bare chest with one hip cocked against the frame. His stance seemed surprisingly relaxed, as if watching her bathe was a part of his daily routine. Joanna was not the least bit relaxed, nor had she been since she'd come upon him in the den cloaked in firelight with his jeans undone to reveal a partial glimpse of the tattoo. And below that, strong evidence that he was aroused. So had she been at that moment. So was she now.

Yet she wasn't exactly surprised by his presence.

After all, this was his private domain and she had left the door partially ajar to keep the bath from steaming up. Or so she'd told herself. In reality, in an inexplicable place buried deep within her psyche, she'd secretly hoped that he would venture inside. Silently yearned for him to shed his clothes, his resistance, and join her for some more water play.

Instead, he continued to stand and stare, and Joanna continued to slowly lather her body with the same soap she had detected on his skin on more than one occasion, as if unaware of his presence.

The simple act of showering took on a whole new meaning. With every stroke over her slick flesh, she imagined his skilled hand there. With every pass over her breasts, she remembered his impassioned touch. With every random tick of her pulse, an all-consuming heat assailed the very core of her. Joanna's head began to whirl with possibilities and her body reeled when she considered where this might lead.

Obviously nowhere, she soon realized after she'd finished washing and he still hadn't made a move. Not even an inch. Maybe he found her figure lacking. Maybe he didn't appreciate the faint stretch marks on her upper thighs, the slight roundness of her belly, the fullness of her hips.

But he'd seen all those details in the hot tub and that hadn't stopped him then. Something was definitely stopping him now.

Resigned that he wasn't going to do anything but gawk, Joanna turned off the spray, pushed open the shower door and grabbed for the bulky black towel hanging on the rack to her left. She dried herself slowly, still very much aware that he continued to study her. But she didn't dare look at him, not yet. Not until after she had her feet firmly planted on the woven mat outside the shower and her robe covering her completely.

Though she felt self-conscious, Joanna affected casualness as she raised her eyes from where she'd cinched the robe's tie loosely around her waist. She met his gaze, dark and intense and oh so seductive. "Did I take too long?" Her voice sounded remarkably nonchalant.

"Not at all." His voice sounded impossibly deep and rough.

"I'll be out of your way in a minute," she said. "Just let me run a quick brush through my hair."

After taking a seat before the vanity, Joanna combed through her unruly curls, not seeing much of anything but Rio's reflection in the wide mirror. His expression remained guarded, still as dispassionate as it had been while he'd watched her bathe, but his eyes belied that appearance of calm and control. They looked dark and disturbed. Very disturbed.

She pivoted on the backless stool to face him with brush in hand and he gave her a slow visual once-over, pausing at her feet. "Your leg's bleeding," he said with a hint of concern.

Joanna sent a quick look down and noticed a thin trail of red oozing from a small cut on her ankle. Great. If she didn't do something about it soon, she would bleed all over the nice beige carpet. "Sorry. I didn't notice." Actually, she had been vaguely aware of the nick while shaving her legs, but the sharp sting had been no match for the mind-numbing ache for Rio's complete attention. It still wasn't.

Reaching behind her, she laid down the brush, snapped a tissue from the holder on the counter and dabbed at the cut.

Without speaking, Rio pushed away from the door and strode toward her, causing her breath to hitch and her heart to leap. He bent and opened the bottom drawer to her left, and as he rummaged through the contents, several items drew Joanna's attention, one in particular. A box of condoms. An industrial-size box.

Rio pushed the box aside, withdrew a bandage and ripped it open then tossed the wrapping into the nearby wastebasket. His mouth formed a grim line as he slammed the drawer and stood in front of her. Joanna expected him to hand her the bandage but instead, he knelt and propped her foot on his leg. She couldn't disregard the fact that she was sitting on a stool wearing only a knee-length pink terry robe with her foot balanced on his taut thigh and her heart lodged in her dry throat. Goose bumps covered her entire body despite the warmth of the bathroom or Rio's heat-inducing gaze now centered on her eyes.

After he gently applied the bandage, Joanna assumed he would stand and leave. But he remained motionless, as if awaiting some sort of response. Joanna supposed she should express her gratitude, verbally thank him, but she couldn't seem to get a handle on her words when he began to brush his thumb over her instep in a maddening rhythm that put her senses on high alert.

Rio continued to silently regard Joanna, the tension as thick as the vapor that had risen from the shower. She had no idea what he was waiting for but she suspected it might be some kind of signal from her, something that indicated she wanted him to act on the electricity arcing between them, and no doubt she did, even though she shouldn't.

But the shouldn'ts and couldn'ts never seemed to matter much when he was around. They didn't matter now as he kept his eyes fastened on her flushed face. She only knew that she wanted him with an urgency that discounted logic.

The last remnants of Joanna's common sense blew away along with any semblance of normal breathing. As if of their own accord, her legs slightly parted and the robe fell to each side of her thighs in blatant invitation.

Without taking his gaze from hers, Rio raised Joanna's foot as well as her heart rate. He planted a soft kiss on her ankle above the bandage, then another on the inside of her calf and after that he moved on to her knee.

Keenly aware of his upward trek and his possible goal, Joanna had a hard time drawing air when he continued his daring exploration. Nothing like kissing and making it better—Joanna's final lucid thought as she clamped her eyes closed while his tongue blazoned a scorching, wet path along her inner thigh. His mouth, so soft upon her naked flesh, generated such a searing heat that she could only consider how badly she needed relief. How badly she needed Rio.

In the distant recesses of her consciousness, Joanna knew it would be wise to halt what he was about to do. But her mind was as weak and shaky as her body, as limp as the sash he untied with one hand as she let him have his way without even one muttered protest. She gripped the edges of the stool when he opened her robe completely, exposing her breasts. At the same time, she opened her eyes to risk a glance, discovering his mouth only inches from intimate terrain.

Joanna couldn't begin to recognize this uninhibited woman residing beneath her skin. The old Joanna would have protested, questioned her wisdom, his intent, or at least looked away. But this newer version couldn't resist Rio Madrid. Couldn't keep from watching, not even after he settled his mouth between her trembling thighs. Not even after he finessed her vulnerable flesh with his clever tongue, stroked her tender breasts with his gifted fingers, continued to scrutinize her as she balanced on the brink of something she wasn't sure she could bear.

Watching the surreal scene, watching him watching her, sent a mind-bending climax tearing through Joanna. The intense sensations made her almost pull away from Rio's provocative torment, but she couldn't. She could only drop her chin to her chest as she rode wave after wave, pulse after pulse of pure bliss.

Before Joanna could completely recover, Rio hauled her into his arms and framed her face in his palms, holding her in place to accept what he so willingly gave—a kiss that threatened to dissolve her where she now stood, a meeting of tongues and teeth and tastes that greatly affected her balance.

Searching for an anchor, she braced her hands on his waist. She needed to feel every part of him, every lovely inch of him, and reached between them to jerk open his fly. When he didn't stop her, she slipped her hand inside his briefs. His hands dropped to her shoulders and he squeezed them tightly when she touched him with firm, inquisitive strokes. Just imagining him inside her made her dizzy, made her some wild, wanton creature.

After Rio groaned, Joanna anticipated he would scoop her up and carry her to his bed, yet he continued to touch her again in much the same way she now touched him, kissed her with unrestrained passion. She was completely and utterly devoid of will. A tiny pinch of apprehension tried to rear its head but Joanna pushed it out of her mind, determined to concentrate solely on her goal, to break Rio down, one touch at a time.

In response, Rio murmured a few words from his mother's native language, phrases he knew Joanna wouldn't understand. Sexual words. His body's reaction needed no interpretation. He was as achingly hard as he'd ever been in his life, as desperate for her as he'd ever been for any woman.

Her smooth, solid caress overrode Rio's resistance, drove him to the brink, sliced his good sense to shreds.

And he couldn't do a damn thing to stop it.

With his mind caught in a carnal haze and his body

screaming for relief, Rio pulled her down onto the bathroom floor and kicked out of his jeans and briefs. He grabbed for a condom from the drawer and hesitated. But that hesitation—that faint glimmer of uncertainty—evaporated when Joanna released a soft beseeching sound.

Rio tore the package open with his teeth and rolled the condom on, then without formality, without the slightest pause, thrust into Joanna's body. The extreme pleasure he felt at that moment came out in a rough sigh as he battled to hang on to his composure, at least for a while longer. Uninhibited, unrestrained, they rolled until Joanna was positioned above him, straddling him, taking the lead that he was more than glad to relinquish. He worked his hands into the damp curls spiraling at her shoulders and kept his eyes fixed firmly on hers, searching for any resistance, for any sign that he had read her wrong. He saw only the perfect portrait of a beautiful, sensual woman caught in a quest for liberation as she moved in an erotic tempo, rode him as if she intended to steal his sanity.

Determined to hold off his climax for as long as he could, Rio nudged Joanna forward with a palm on her back until he could take her pink-tipped breast into his mouth. He clasped her hips and gently pushed her down until he immersed himself completely in her inviting heat. She straightened and tilted her head back, her eyes closed, her lips trembling. Rio sensed she was on the verge of another orgasm. He wasn't very far behind.

Beyond that point, Rio stopped thinking, stopped considering anything but the raw passion that blocked everything from his brain as a climax ripped through him, took him beyond the realm of conscious thought where nothing existed but Joanna's own climax pulling him deeper inside her body, deeper into mindlessness.

After a time, Joanna wilted against his chest and her breath came out in ragged gasps to match his own. Rio held her tightly, reveling in the clean rain-shower scent emanating from her silky hair and soft skin, the taste of her still lingering on his tongue and lips. He experienced every brisk beat of her heart against his chest and each lingering pulsation where they were still joined. But as the sensations began to subside, awareness struck him like a fist in the face.

Joanna Blake was more than he'd ever imagined her to be as a lover, even in his most untamed dreams. Regardless of what she'd done to his body, done to his mind, it couldn't compare to the havoc she was creating in his heart. She had set free something in him that he'd never expected, something far removed from physical gratification, and he knew in an elemental way he would never be the same from this point forward.

He also recognized that she needed more than sex. She needed a man who could love her well, day in and day out. A steady secure man who didn't mind giving up his freedom to settle into a normal routine. He wasn't sure he would ever be able to open himself up to the possibility of a lifelong commitment, even if Joanna was the only woman who'd ever come close to rousing those feelings within him. Feelings he was too damn afraid to acknowledge.

With so many concerns hanging over his head, Rio began to regret giving in to base urges. He admittedly enjoyed sex hot and hard and fast if the situation called for it. And yes, Joanna had willingly participated, but she hadn't exactly asked him, at least not verbally.

But this was more than sex. More than he cared to

deal with at the moment. He had to come to terms with the fact that he'd started it, something he'd sworn not to do, and he'd finished it without regard to what she needed—slow, tender, considerate lovemaking in a comfortable bed, not on a bathroom floor, especially not the first time.

Right now he had to get away from her so he could think. So he could sufficiently chastise himself for the loss of control. He didn't like losing control.

As much as he wanted to take Joanna to his bed, to say to hell with work and make love to her all day long, he wouldn't. Not if he intended to face the harsh reality of the situation—she deserved better than him.

Slowly Rio rolled her aside, breaking all intimate contact, leaving him feeling oddly bereft. He came to his feet and started toward the door, his limbs heavy with satisfaction, his head and heart burdened with guilt.

Without retrieving his clothes, without even a glance back, he muttered, "I'm sorry."

Seven

Sorry?

Joanna could only stare mutely at Rio's strong back as he left the room, left her lying naked on the floor with her mouth agape and her body still shaking from their lovemaking.

Lovemaking? Not hardly, she thought. Sex would be a more accurate description. Wicked, fast, incredible sex. Except for one thing. When Rio had slid inside her body, he'd managed to work his way further into her heart. And she hated that, hated that she'd left herself so open, so vulnerable to a man who had promised her nothing beyond a place to live and a vow that they would be lovers. Now they were lovers, and he was sorry.

Snatching her robe from the floor, Joanna shrugged it on and secured the belt at her waist so tightly she thought she might cut off the circulation from her neck to her ribs. With determined steps, she walked into his bedroom to find him stretched out on his back on the bed beneath a sheet—a black satin sheet that sheltered only his groin and left leg, leaving his chest exposed as well as the rigid plane of his abdomen. His other leg, bent at the knee, revealed the distinct, solid muscle defining his calf and thigh, both covered in a fine veneer of dark, masculine hair.

Joanna forced her gaze to Rio's face where he had an arm draped over his eyes, his dark hair a near match to the sleek black pillow. Even now, even though she could probably spit nails because of his sudden departure, desire shot back to life, threatening to urge her forward into his bed, into his arms to invite him back inside her body.

With all the strength she could muster, Joanna hugged her arms to her middle in order to resist him. But she refused to leave until she'd said her piece. "Do you mind explaining what that was all about?"

"You know what that was all about." His voice sounded coarse, either from the lack of sleep or an abundance of regret.

"I'm not talking about the sex, Rio. I'm talking about you running away with nothing more than some lame apology."

He dropped his arm from his eyes yet failed to look at anything but the ceiling. "I apologize again. I should never have allowed that to happen."

She should never have let him into her life, much less into her heart. "You weren't exactly alone in there. And if you'll recall, I didn't stop you."

"You didn't ask me, either."

Frustration brought fire to Joanna's cheeks. "Was I supposed to say, 'Rio, take me now'? I think it was more than obvious that I wanted it to happen."

He turned to his side to face her, his elbow bent and his palm providing support for his jaw. The sheet slipped lower, revealing a glimpse of the mat of dark hair below his navel and the jaguar. Only a microinch more, and Joanna would be able to see everything that made Rio Madrid undeniably male. Moments ago, she had gained personal, intimate knowledge of that part of him, and she'd been anything but disappointed. Her pulse sprinted with the remembrance of how glorious it had felt to have him fill her completely. She wanted to relive it again. Here. Now.

Joanna clenched her jaw, angered by her sudden lack of self-discipline. What on earth was wrong with her? She was supposed to be mad at him, furious even. She wasn't supposed to want him, but regretfully she still did.

He settled his golden gaze on her eyes. "You deserve more than a quick roll, Joanna."

"I deserve some honesty, Rio. Some respect."

"It's because I respect you that I'm feeling pretty damn guilty at the moment." He rolled onto his back and sent one large palm slowly down his chest, bringing it to rest over the jaguar below his belly, as if he and that powerful symbol were truly one. "If I hadn't left when I did, I ran the risk of losing control again."

Joanna's mood brightened somewhat, knowing that he hadn't been disappointed by the experience. Knowing he had wanted her as much as she'd wanted him, at least from a physical standpoint. "And what exactly is wrong with losing control? Does that make you too human?"

"It makes me less of a man because I didn't stop to consider what you need. But when I watched you bathing, touching yourself in the shower, I couldn't think beyond what I wanted—to finally be inside you even if it meant taking you on a bathroom floor.'' He released a humorless laugh. ''Not one of my finer moments.''

Joanna would have to argue that, but she wouldn't do anything to nourish his ego. ''Why can't we just chalk it up to pure animal lust?'' The words sounded hollow, even to her own ears. It hadn't been that simple, at least not for her.

Rio sent a glance her way before returning his sullen gaze back to the ceiling. ''In my experience, I've learned that women are brave beyond all bounds, stronger than most men in many instances. They deserve to be treated with the utmost respect.'' He turned his head toward her. ''You're a single mother, Joanna. You have a responsibility to your son as well as to yourself. You don't need to be involved with someone like me.''

''Then you're saying you're not worthy?''

''I'm saying that I probably can't give you what you need beyond sex. Do you really want to settle for only that?''

Joanna didn't know what she wanted at the moment. She only knew that when she was with him, no matter what the circumstance, she experienced some sort of spiritual connection. That in itself was ill advised, something that had become painfully obvious the moment Rio had admitted that he could offer her nothing more than a little sexual satisfaction. A *quick roll* now and then.

Weary and exhausted, she saw no reason to continue a conversation that would get them nowhere, at least not now. She needed to go to work, fulfill her responsibilities, leave Rio to his remorse while she dealt with her own. She had to learn to accept him for who he was—a man who wanted no ties, a man very much like her ex-husband in that regard though that's where the similarity ended. Still, she couldn't make those same mistakes again, not when it came to her threadbare heart and her son's welfare.

Tipping up her chin, shoring up her frame, she dropped her hands to her sides and fisted the robe in a death grip. "Now that you've cleared everything up, I'll get ready for work. We can forget this ever happened." She would never forget. Ever.

As she turned away, he caught her hand, jolting her, unnerving her, but she didn't dare face him.

"I wish things were different, Joanna, and maybe someday you'll understand." His voice held a trace of sadness, of regret. "But right now, you only have to understand one thing. I can't remember ever wanting a woman as much as I want you." When his warm lips slid over her wrist, a flash of memory, sharp as a needle stick, bolted into Joanna's brain—the memory of his mouth caressing her thoroughly. Every part of her.

It would be so effortless to give into those memories, to go to him and experience each one again. To accept the fact that he could give her everything she desired when it came to lovemaking, yet he couldn't give her love.

In the silence of the room, with her hand still steadfastly wrapped in his hand, her life reluctantly meshed with his life, she secretly admitted that a part of her needed his love.

Pulling from his grasp, Joanna rushed back to her room, away from him. As she had that first night in the ballroom, she instinctively knew that she might never escape the hold he had on her, no matter how far or how fast she ran.

Rio had opted to drive to the hospital on the bike this morning in hopes that some cold air might clear his head. It hadn't. Now in the process of making morning rounds, the mental fog cluttering his mind wouldn't dissipate, even after two cups of espresso he'd made at home and one mudlike cup of coffee he'd managed to gulp down in the doctors' lounge.

Exhaustion wasn't hindering his thought processes; Joanna was. He couldn't halt the guilt trip he seemed determined to take. He couldn't shake what had happened between them earlier. Nor could he stop thinking he wanted it to happen again.

Right now he had to quit considering everything but his duty to his patients.

He strode down the hospital corridor running on autopilot. When he arrived at his destination, he snapped the chart from outside the door and pushed his way into the room. The woman whose baby he'd delivered only a few hours ago looked up from the bed expectantly.

Though she appeared thoroughly worn out, she managed a bright grin. "Good morning, Dr. Madrid."

He returned a courteous smile that felt much too forced. "How are you doing, Mrs. Rutherford?"

"I'm doing great, but I'd be even better if they'd bring me my baby."

Rio glanced at the empty crib near the bed. "Have you seen him since the delivery?"

"No, but the nurse told me that right after they had him bathed and dressed, they'd bring him right in."

"How long ago was that?"

She glanced at the wall clock. "About two hours ago, I think. I drifted off. I do hope they bring him soon because my husband's coming back before he has to leave for work. He's bringing our daughter."

Rio dropped the chart on the bedside table and said, "I'll be right back."

Returning to the hallway, he dashed to the nurses' station and found the charge nurse charting at the desk. "Sara, do you know why the Rutherford baby hasn't been brought to his mother?"

The woman looked up and shrugged. "Sorry. I didn't know he hadn't been. She's not my patient. We've been swamped since the shift change."

Rio was swamped by sudden anger. But he reined in his temper knowing she didn't warrant his frustration. "The mother is breast-feeding," he said, taking the edge from his voice. "Mind calling the nursery to find out what's going on?"

"Sure, Dr. Madrid. Anything else?"

"Nope, that's it."

Her gray eyes narrowed and she frowned. "Rough night?"

Rough morning. "Just the usual."

She closed the chart and gave him her full attention. "Well, I hope you get some rest this weekend. We've got a full moon on Monday. You know what that means."

Yeah, he knew what full moons meant. All hell breaking loose in the baby department. He thought about his mother, in part because Sara reminded him somewhat of her—kind eyes and a worldly wisdom—but anytime he considered the moon, he thought of her. She'd wholeheartedly believed in the powers of the universe, legends learned from her Mayan heritage, but most of all she believed in the infinite power of love. And she'd loved Rio's stepfather, though God only knew why. The man had been anything but lovable.

He sent Sara a brief smile and a muttered, "Thanks," then headed away.

An unexpected sadness settled over Rio as he walked

the quiet corridor. An overwhelming feeling of loss, but he considered that it only had to do in part with his mother, and more to do with losing Joanna. That realization made him take a mental step back. You couldn't lose something you've never really had, he decided. And he couldn't have Joanna, not beyond what they had shared this morning.

By the time he made it back to his patient, Mr. Rutherford had returned to his wife with their five-year-old-daughter in tow. Rutherford stuck out his beefy hand. "Great to see you, Dr. Madrid. Thanks for everything you did last night."

Rio took the hand he offered for a quick, robust shake. "Your wife did all the work. I was just there to make the catch."

Both Mr. and Mrs. Rutherford chuckled while their frowning daughter looked on, twirling a blond curl around her finger with a vengeance.

The door swung open to a nurse carrying a yellow bundle in her arms.

"Looks like the guest of honor has finally arrived," Rio said. After he took the newborn from her, the nurse rushed away as if she expected he might take her head off. Obviously Sara had read the staff the riot act over not bringing the child in sooner.

Rio approached the bed to finally unite child with mother but first caught a glimpse of round cheeks and sleepy innocence from beneath the blanket. Another bout of melancholy crept in as he laid the baby in Mrs. Rutherford's arms.

"Does he have a name yet?" Rio asked.

"Rufus Harold Jr.," Mr. Rutherford stated with open pride.

Rufus Rutherford. Tough break, Rio thought. "And

you are?'' he asked the little girl who seemed totally disinterested in her brother, if not somewhat annoyed.

She jutted out her chin in defiance. ''Rita Louise Rutherford and I don't like babies.''

''Rita,'' Mrs. Rutherford scolded. ''You haven't even seen him yet. Come take a look.''

''I don't wanna.''

A classic case of sibling rivalry, Rio decided. When Mr. Rutherford stepped forward as if to escort his daughter out, Rio put up a hand to stop him then pulled a lollipop from his lab-coat pocket and offered it to Rita. ''For the big sister.''

She seemed somewhat appeased yet still not overly thrilled as she unwrapped the candy and stuck it in her mouth. Rio knelt on her level. ''My mother spoke often about the sun and moon. The sun is strong and therefore in charge of looking after the moon.'' He brushed away a golden curl from her shoulder. ''Since your hair is the color of the sun, then your little brother will be the moon. He'll look to you for guidance. That's a very important job. Think you can do that, Rita?''

She glanced over her shoulder toward the baby then pulled the sucker from her mouth with a pop. ''I guess so, as long as he doesn't get into my stuff.''

Rio presented his first real smile of the day when Rita gave him a winning grin. ''Why don't you try holding him?''

After Rita nodded and handed her father the candy, Rio picked her up and put her on the bed. Mrs. Rutherford gently placed the baby in his sister's arms and Rio saw an immediate transformation in the little girl. New life had a way of working on a person, no matter what that person's age.

Mrs. Rutherford looked up with a grateful expression. "Thank you, Dr. Madrid."

"No problem, and I'm sorry it took so long for you have your son with you."

While Rita continued to hold the baby, Mrs. Rutherford unwrapped the blanket to do the usual motherly all-parts-accounted-for check. "Two hours is a long time to be without your child."

Try two months, Rio thought as Joanna's predicament worked its way back into his brain. As he watched the family gathered around to survey the miracle, he realized how much Joanna needed to have her son with her.

He'd been alone for so long, Rio was only beginning to realize the importance of that concept—and the extent of his own loneliness. He hadn't stopped to consider how difficult it must be for Joanna, not having those she loved and needed nearby. He'd only considered how much he wanted her, his own desires and needs. That made him a selfish bastard, and somehow, someway, he needed to make amends.

Starting now.

Joanna dismissed her next-to-last patient and moved on to the final one, thankful to discover the patient was Allison Cartwright. She could use a familiar face right now, someone who might distract her from thoughts of Rio.

As Joanna entered the exam room, Allison smiled but it immediately faded. "You look absolutely beat, Joanna."

She felt as if she'd taken a beating—to her heart. "It's been a long day." Joanna moved to the chair next to the table where Allison sat wearing a cornflower-blue exam gown, her swollen feet propped up on a stool. ''How have you been feeling?''

''Pretty good, except for the usual pregnancy woes. Caroline examined me since you were running behind.''

Joanna tamped down her guilt. ''I'm sorry. I'm not moving very fast today. Anything special to report?''

Allison's smile disappeared. ''Actually, she's a little concerned about my blood pressure.''

Flipping open the chart, Joanna scanned the notes. ''Your pressure is a bit high but your urine looks normal for now. However, you do have quite a bit of edema.'' She set the chart down and turned her attention to Allison. ''To be on the safe side, I'm going to put you on bed rest for the next couple of weeks. I also want to check you on Monday, and in the meantime, we'll order a few lab tests.''

Allison's eyes widened. ''Bed rest? Is that necessary? I really don't have any extra sick leave coming to me. If I have to take off early then I run the risk of losing my job.''

''Allison, I know it's tough, but I don't want to run the risk of anything happening to you or your baby. You could be facing preeclampsia and we don't want to take any chances. Preeclampsia is a condition where—''

''I know all about it,'' Allison said. ''My sister had it and so did my mother. In fact, my mother died giving birth to my sister from full-blown eclampsia.''

Joanna's concern increased. ''I'm so sorry to hear that, Allison. And that's all the more reason to watch you carefully since you could have a genetic predisposition.''

Allison sighed. ''Okay, I'll figure something out. This baby is very important to me and I don't want to take any chances whatsoever. After all, the doctors said I'd never be able to get pregnant.''

Joanna smiled. ''Well, I guess they were wrong, weren't they?''

''Yes, they were, and speaking of doctors, I spoke to Dr. Madrid today.''

Joanna swallowed hard. ''Really?''

''Yes, on the phone, and I appreciate you letting him know about my decision.''

''He seemed okay with it?''

''Yeah, he was fine, as far as I could tell.''

Joanna wondered how cooperative Rio would be if he knew of Allison's current problems. ''I'm glad.''

''He did seem a little distracted, though.''

He could join the club, Joanna thought. ''I'm sure he's probably very busy.''

''He said I was in good hands with you.'' Allison grinned. ''Does he have personal knowledge of your hands?''

Boy, did he. ''Very funny, Allison.''

''I'm sorry, but that day I saw him here at the center, I could tell something was going on between you two.''

Joanna's face felt like an inferno. ''What makes you think that?''

''By the way he looked at you. Are you going to deny there's something going on between you two?''

After hesitating just a little too long, Joanna realized she might as well come clean. After all, she could use someone to talk to. Several times she'd almost called Cassie O'Connor but she didn't want to burden a busy mother of twins. And she *had* forged a friendship with Allison in the past few weeks. Right now Joanna could use a friend. A female friend.

Turning away from Allison, Joanna walked to the

counter and toyed with the chart. ''Actually, I live with Rio.''

Allison's sharp intake of air caused Joanna to face her once more. ''I had no idea it was that serious,'' Allison said.

''I'm only living with him temporarily until I can find a decent place of my own.''

''But there's a little more to it, isn't there?''

Joanna lowered her eyes and fiddled with the stethoscope hanging around her neck. ''I suppose you could say that.''

''Are you sharing his bed?''

Maybe not his bed, but she had shared his bathroom floor. ''I guess you could say things have progressed from an intimate standpoint. Right now I'm kind of confused over the whole situation.''

''Sex can definitely cause confusion. It certainly changes things.''

''Yes, it does,'' Joanna said.

Joanna glanced up to see Allison's hands resting on her distended belly, regarding her with a questioning gaze. ''Are you in love with him, Joanna?''

Hearing the words sent shock waves spiraling through Joanna. ''I'm, um, well, I'm very fond of him.''

Allison's eyes went wide. ''God, you *are* in love with him, aren't you? Didn't they teach you in school to never fall for a doctor?''

Joanna had sworn to never fall in love again, probably an unrealistic goal unless she decided to stop living completely. But she certainly hadn't intended to take that leap now, and especially not with a man like Rio Madrid. A man who steered clear of commitment. ''I'm not in love with him.'' Yet.

''Are you sure?''

"Of course." Liar. "Believe me, I've worked with more than a few doctors that are great at what they do, attractive in a lot of ways and anything but commitment material." Rio in a nutshell.

"So have I," Allison said wistfully. "And it's the hardest thing to accept, isn't it?"

Joanna was beginning to suspect Allison had more than a little personal experience with doctors. "Stop me if I'm being too intrusive, but does a doctor figure into your baby's parentage?"

After glancing at the picture of a perfect family hanging on the pale-blue wall, Allison turned sad eyes back to Joanna. "Yes, my baby's father happens to be a doctor."

"Does he know about the pregnancy?" Joanna asked.

Allison twisted the hem on the gown until Joanna thought it might rip. "No, not yet."

"Are you going to tell him?"

"I'm not sure. He's only recently returned from a six-month leave of absence. I don't know how he would take the news or if he would even want to be involved. It happened one night, a huge mistake, except for the pregnancy. I wouldn't take that back for a minute. This baby is a miracle."

Joanna's heart went out to Allison knowing she might have to raise a child alone. How well she could relate to that. And although she was curious to know exactly who the unidentified doctor might be, she wouldn't ask. "Right now, let's concentrate on your health. Get plenty of rest, we'll monitor you carefully and by this time next month, you'll have your little one. Then you can decide what you want to do about the father."

Allison sent Joanna a knowing smile. "And maybe

soon you'll have what you want, too. Whatever that might be."

Right now Joanna only wanted to go home and consider what she needed to do about Rio. At least it was Friday and she wasn't scheduled to take call but she did intend to phone her son. She needed to hear his voice, to speak to the little man, the center of her life, the only male who should matter at the moment. And Joseph did matter, more than anything in the universe. But one thing had become all too apparent. Despite how angry he'd made her that morning, Rio Madrid was starting to matter to Joanna. Too much.

Eight

At a little past 8:00 p.m., Joanna arrived home and held her breath as she pulled up behind Rio's truck. In a way she'd hoped to find him gone. Another part of her warred with excitement just knowing he was there.

"I'm mad at you, Rio," she murmured as she turned off the ignition and slid out of the sedan. She continued her litany as she strode up the front walkway. "Very angry. Furious, in fact. Absolutely livid—"

"Mama!"

Joanna's mouth dropped open at the same time she dropped her keys and purse onto the walk. Before she could quite register the sight of her son running toward her from the house, Joseph had already hurled himself at her waist in an enthusiastic embrace. Tears of pure joy rushed in and a boulder-size lump formed in Joanna's throat as she knelt to hold her precious baby in her arms. She brushed the dark hair from his forehead and replaced it with kiss after kiss until Joseph pulled away and said, "You're getting me all wet, Mama."

"I'm sorry, but I've missed you so much, honey." She swiped an arm over her damp face then immediately wrapped it back around him. "What are you doing here?"

Joseph grinned and in the diffused light coming from the porch, she could see the dark space where he had lost his first tooth in her absence. "Mr. Rio put me and Gran on a plane so we could come see you this weekend."

"Oh he did, did he?" Joanna was so utterly surprised by the gesture, so totally grateful to Rio that her anger died like fall foliage in winter. "That was very nice of him," she managed to say through a sniff. "Where's Gran?"

"In the house with Mr. Rio."

Joanna grabbed up her belongings and took Joseph's hand, relishing the feel of his tiny fingers wrapped around hers. Oh, how she had missed him. "He's a doctor, sweetie, not a mister. Dr. Madrid."

Joseph shrugged and skipped along the path, dragging Joanna with him. "He said I could call him Rio, but Gran always says you should call someone mister if you don't know him."

"If he told you to call him Rio, then you can do that."

Only a few moments before, Joanna had wanted to call Rio much worse. Now she only wanted to thank him and hug him for doing something so totally incredible as reuniting mother and son.

Once in the foyer, Joanna found her mother waiting for her at the entry to the den, her light-blue eyes still vibrant and full of mischief despite her advancing age, her silver hair still styled in the same short casual cut, as it had been for as long as Joanna could remember.

She opened her arms to Joanna. "Hello there, daughter dear."

Joanna relinquished Joseph in order to hug her mother hard. She fought another bout of tears with great effort as she kissed her cheek. "You really pulled a fast one this time, Margaret Ann Mathis. I can't remember when I've had such a welcome surprise."

Margaret patted Joanna's cheek. "You have Dr. Madrid to thank for that. He actually persuaded me to get on a plane. Can you imagine that?"

Joanna wasn't at all surprised. Rio could be very persuasive. She glanced beyond her mother and visually searched the den but found it deserted. "Where is the doctor, anyway?"

"He's in the garage. He said he'd stay out of the way until we had a chance to say our hellos. I told him that wasn't necessary, but he insisted. He also insisted on having dinner brought in. I hope you don't mind, but we've already eaten. Joseph was starving and Rio wasn't certain when you'd be home. We saved you some."

"That's okay. I'm not really hungry." She wanted to find Rio, to thank him properly. "Why don't I see if he'll join us? We can have a nice visit before Joseph's bedtime."

"I'm not sleepy," Joseph said adamantly as he bent and hugged Gabby who had come into the foyer to check out the happenings. The dog wagged her tail furiously and licked Joseph's face until the boy fell into a fit of giggles.

Gabby had never paid Joanna much mind. Obviously the dog was quite taken with both Joanna's men.

Both her men…

But Rio wasn't hers.

"While you go and get the doctor, I'll put Joseph in the tub," Margaret said.

Joanna nodded toward the stairs. "There's a really nice old bathtub up in my room. Joseph will love it. Through the door at the top of the—"

"I know." Margaret patted her arm. "Rio gave us the grand tour. He said that Joseph and I could have his room and he'll sleep on the twin in the guest room."

"I wanna sleep with Mama," Joseph said. "In Rio's room."

Joanna ruffled his hair. "That's fine, Joseph. As long as you don't steal all the covers or kick me out of the bed."

"Then I'll take your room, Joanna. Now you run along and go find your young man."

Better to set her mother straight immediately, Joanna decided. Before she got the wrong idea. "He's not my young man, Mom. He's my landlord."

Margaret flipped a hand of dismissal toward Joanna and sent her a smile that said she believed otherwise. "Whatever you say, my dear." She held out her hand to Joseph. "Come along, tough stuff. Time to get cleaned up."

Joseph ran back to Joanna and hugged her around the waist, then set off with his grandmother up the stairs. Joanna took a minute to watch them as they made their way to the second floor where Joseph paused at the stained-glass window and said, "Cool." Joanna smiled, still not quite believing they were here, in the flesh, thanks to Rio.

On that thought, she headed through the kitchen and outside toward the detached garage. She noted a sliver of light coming from beneath the closed entry door and heard the sound of a blaring classic-rock song. She knocked on the side door twice and after receiving no response, concluded that Rio couldn't hear anything over the din. She entered to find him sitting cross-legged beside a shiny black motorcycle, oblivious to her presence.

He wore a pair of tattered faded jeans and an equally faded blue T-shirt that read, Let the Power Consume You. And boy, did she ever feel consumed by his power while watching him tightening some sort of bolt near the bike's rear tire. The tendons in his forearms flexed as he worked and Joanna was as mesmerized now as she had been the time she'd watched him perform the C-section on Mrs. Gonzales. Everything he did with his hands seemed effortless, especially when he'd used them on her.

Images drifted into her mind of that morning, images of kisses and caresses, bodies entwined…

She tried to shut them off at the same time she shut off the radio positioned on a worktable to her right. The music abruptly stopped but to her chagrin, the memories did not.

Rio glanced up, confusion in his expression until he pinned her in place with his hypnotist's eyes. "Sorry, I didn't know you were there," he said as he unfolded and stood, grabbed a rag from a nearby shelf then began wiping his hands.

Joanna walked a little closer and surveyed his work. "What are you doing?"

"Just a few minor adjustments. I ran over a curb today on the way to the hospital. Guess I wasn't paying attention. But I've almost got it fixed."

Joanna was surprised she hadn't taken out a few trees on her way to work after their morning together. She caught a whiff of his trademark exotic scent mixed with a faint hint of grease and quelled the urge to launch herself into his strong arms, much the same as Joseph had with her. "Just wanted to let you know that your presence has been requested in the house by our surprise guests."

He continued to wipe the black-brown smudges from his hands as a smile played at the corners of his sensuous mouth. "Hope you didn't mind me inviting them here without your consent."

"Mind? I'm ecstatic. I'm also in awe that you managed to get them here without my knowledge. How did you know where to find them?"

"It wasn't difficult considering you have the address and phone number taped to the refrigerator." He gave her a one-shoulder shrug and tossed the rag aside. "It was a spur-of-the-moment thing. I decided you could use some company."

At the moment she could use a little fortitude, because right now she really wanted to thank him for his efforts in a few decidedly wicked ways.

She opted to hug him, engage him in an innocent embrace. Stepping forward, she wrapped her arms around his waist then stood on tiptoe and whispered in his ear, "Thank you, Rio."

He responded with only a murmured, "I'm going to get you dirty, Joanna."

She tipped her head back and stared up at him but didn't let him go. "I don't care. I'm just happy and grateful for what you've done."

Finally his arms—warm and solid and strong—circled her, drew her closer. "My pleasure."

That simple word *pleasure* seemed to take on a life of its own in the empty garage, and Joanna, ignoring every caution bouncing around in her brain, pressed her lips against his.

She wasn't at all sure what to expect from Rio, maybe even a rejection. What she got was a kiss that could melt the motorcycle. He tasted like cherry-flavored candy, sweet and sensual and seductive as he swept his tongue inside her mouth in a slow, scorching rhythm. Joanna forgot what she'd come for—to thank him verbally and nothing more. Totally forgot herself.

She sent her hands on a journey over his back, delighting in the feel of corded muscle against the damp T-shirt. Rio's hands traveled to her hips where he nudged her forward. Without breaking the kiss, he turned her around and backed her up against the utility shelf. Several items fell to the floor in a noisy clatter but it wasn't enough to part them, or to stop Rio from slipping his hands up her sides and sending brush strokes along the outer rim of her breasts with his thumbs.

Joanna knew they should stop now—*she* should stop him—but short of an earthquake, it wasn't very likely that was going to happen.

''Mama?''

After a moment of shock, Joanna ducked under Rio's arm to find Joseph standing at the door looking faintly surprised and more than a little curious. She shoved her hair away from her face and tried to appear nonchalant. ''Hi, sweetie. I thought you were taking a bath.''

Joseph's gaze wandered past Joanna, she presumed to home in on Rio. ''Gran wants to know where we can find clean towels.''

Joanna glanced at Rio over one shoulder as if she had no idea what a towel was, much less where her son could find one.

Rio cleared his throat. ''I have extras in my bathroom. Or there're a few in a basket in the laundry room.''

Joanna nodded. ''Yes, in the laundry room. I washed some but I haven't had a chance to put them away.''

Joseph backed out the door, flashed them a huge grin then spun and ran toward the house.

Joanna grabbed her nape and closed her eyes. ''Oh, God. I can't believe that just happened.''

''Us kissing or your son catching us kissing?''

''Both.''

Rio's palms rested on her shoulders from behind as she opened her eyes to stare out the door, half expecting her mother to come marching in to see what the heck was going on.

''I'm sorry we got caught,'' he said in a low, controlled voice. ''I can't say I'm sorry you kissed me.''

She shrugged off his hands and faced him, angry once more, this time at herself. ''You don't have anything to be sorry for. I'm the one who started it.''

''You didn't hear me protest, did you?''

Forking both hands through her hair, she sighed. ''What is it with me, anyway? What is it with us?''

Rio hooked his thumbs in the pockets of his jeans, drawing Joanna's attention to the obvious ridge beneath the denim. ''When two people are as attracted to each other as we seem to be, it's bound to happen.''

She pulled her gaze back to his face. ''It's not normal. Not for me, anyway.''

''Oh, it's normal, all right. You've never wanted to acknowledge it before.''

Not before him. ''If you say so.''

He studied her straight on. ''Do you really think Joseph's going to have a problem with it?''

"I don't know. He's never even seen me with a man, much less seen me kissing one."

"Maybe it's time he understands that his mother might need someone else's company aside from his."

"I don't want him or my mother thinking—"

"That you're involved with someone like me?"

The hurt in his tone took Joanna aback. "I don't want them to know that I'm involved with anyone. They might make more out of it than they should." Joanna was battling that very thing where Rio was concerned.

"Maybe you're vying for sainthood."

"That's not what I'm doing."

"Are you sure?"

"I can't believe you'd ask me that after this morning. I acted anything but saintly."

He grinned. "I can't really argue that. But then I wasn't likely to win any medals in the saint department either."

Joanna tried to force her smile away but it came calling despite her efforts to hold it back. "I guess you could say both of us were feeling a bit sinful."

"You felt damn good, if you ask me. Tasted good, too."

"So did you," Joanna said on a breathy whisper.

Turning back to the bike, Rio reclaimed his place on the ground. "Go back inside, Joanna. Before I..." He picked up a wrench without looking at her.

"Before you what?"

"Before I lay you down on this concrete floor for a little horizontal Olympics."

Joanna shivered at the thought, and it wasn't from the cold air filtering through the open door. She felt as if she were balanced on a tightrope, poised to fall at any given moment. No doubt they wanted each other with a passion that crushed common sense on a regular basis. Still, she had to remember that great sex was all that existed between them, was all that would ever exist. Rio had made that quite clear.

She also needed to remember that Joseph was now present and he didn't need to believe that Rio would be a constant in their lives. Come summer, she should have enough money to find her own place, to move on. God help them all if Joseph should become too attached to the doctor. God help her if she did the same.

With her hand braced on the doorknob, she paused to make a very important declaration. "I think it's best if we just try to stay away from each other until my mom and Joseph leave."

Rio glanced up at her, the wrench poised in one hand. "And after that?"

"I don't know." And she didn't.

He went back to tinkering with the bolt. "As I've said before, you'll have to come to me."

"That's interesting. I don't remember it being that way at all this morning."

His gaze snapped to hers. "This morning was an exception. From now on, it's entirely up to you."

Big, tough Rio, she wanted to say, but she only sent him a hard look that he didn't notice due to his preoccupation with his repairs. He might pretend to have all the strength in the world, but she was beginning to know better, at least when it came to their mutual desire. Joanna wasn't all that strong either, which meant anything could happen from this point forward. And though it might not be a good idea to find her way into Rio's bed, the thought was all too tempting.

An hour later, Joanna prepared to find her way into Rio's bed—to keep company with her son. As she came out of the bathroom, she found Joseph examining several items on the small table situated in front of the black sofa in the bedroom's sitting area. He picked up a small crystal figurine in the shape of a jungle cat and held it up for examination.

"Be careful, Joseph. We don't want to break anything."

Joseph set the statue down gingerly then turned and bounded into the bed. "How come Rio likes cats?" he asked as he crawled beneath the covers.

Joanna stretched out on the bed and turned on her side to face him. "It's part of his culture."

Joseph frowned. "Huh?"

"His mother was descended from the Mayan people in Mexico and they believe animals are special."

"Oh." Joseph plopped back on the pillow. "I think animals are special, too. Can we go to the zoo tomorrow?"

She laid an arm above his head. "That sounds like a plan."

Joseph yawned. "I really like Rio. Do you like Rio?"

She stroked his fine, dark hair. "Yes, I do."

"Is that why you were kissing him?"

Here it comes. "Yes. Does that bother you, sweetie?"

"I think it's kind of yucky."

Joanna chuckled. "You probably won't when you get older."

He wrinkled his nose as if she'd said he would learn to like zucchini. "I don't think so."

Joseph sounded so certain, so much older than his six years, bringing about Joanna's wistful smile. "Well, you've got plenty of time to decide. Right now you need to go to sleep." She reached over and snapped off the bedside lamp—shrouding the room in darkness—then settled her head onto the pillow. She immediately detected Rio's distinctive scent and felt oddly comforted by it. A strong sense of yearning washed over her, a longing that had more to do with emotional needs than those of the flesh. She couldn't afford to want that much from him. He couldn't give her that kind of commitment.

Besides, she had her son, and that's all she really needed.

"Mama?"

"Yes?"

"I like Rio a lot."

So did she. A whole lot. "Good. Sleep tight."

"Mama, one more thing."

"Okay, one more thing."

"Am I ever going to get a real dad?"

Joanna's heart began to hurt over such a simple yet complex question. She had no idea how to answer. No idea at all. "If I find someone whom I think would be a good dad for you, you'll be the first to know."

He sighed. "Okay, but I think Rio would make a real good daddy."

Rio had no idea why he was doing it, only that he couldn't seem to stop. Everywhere they'd gone today, he couldn't maintain control of his hands. At the zoo, he'd found himself holding on to Joanna's elbow with some sort of primal male possessiveness. On the Riverwalk, he'd taken one of her hands into his when Joseph had taken the other, as if they were a typical family on a Saturday stroll. At the Tex-Mex restaurant, he'd inadvertently laid his palm on Joanna's thigh beneath the table as if he had a right to do so. He certainly had to hand it to her—not once had she slapped him. Or stopped him.

Rio had noticed a few covert looks from Joanna's mom—knowing looks. Still, he liked Margaret a lot. She'd been amusing, friendly and she'd shown a great deal of concern for Joanna without being overbearing. And Joseph—well, the kid was great. Rio saw Joanna's strength in him although he was much more outgoing. But then Joanna had been gregarious during their outing and he suspected that had to do with her family's presence. She'd also seemed more relaxed. Unfortunately Rio wasn't relaxed, then or now.

As tired as he'd been, both from an inability to catch up on lost sleep but also from wrestling with a six-year-old several times during the day, he'd agreed to play some video games with Joseph. And after that, he'd agreed to watch an action-packed video involving martial arts and bad jokes.

Now here they were, boy and man, stretched out on their bellies across the den floor. Somewhere midpoint in the movie, Joseph had fallen asleep with his arm around Gabby who, too, was snoozing away.

"Looks like he's down for the count," Joanna said from above him.

Rio stretched and sat up to face her, every muscle in his body protesting the position he'd maintained for over two hours. But certain parts definitely came awake when he noticed Joanna's shower-damp hair and the robe she now wore, the same one she'd worn yesterday morning.

She'd been scarce most of the evening, engaged in conversation in the kitchen with her mother. And she looked happier than she'd looked since he'd met her. He liked that, seeing her happy. He liked making her happy, a thought that jumped into his brain unexpectedly. One he would take out and analyze later.

"He hasn't moved an inch since the bad guys took one of the good guys hostage," Rio said with a wry grin.

"I'll wake him so I can get him in bed."

"I'll take care of it." Rio gently rolled Joseph over then slipped his arms beneath him. The boy opened his eyes but only for a brief moment before closing them again. Rio carried him up the stairs with little effort, surprised by the strange feelings that ran through him when Joseph wrapped his thin arms around his neck, amazed that something so foreign as carrying a sleeping child to bed would actually feel so right.

When they made it to Rio's bedroom, Margaret was waiting outside the door. "I'll sleep with him tonight, Joanna. In your room, if Rio doesn't mind climbing a few more stairs."

"I don't mind at all," Rio said.

Joanna's staid expression said that she minded. "That's okay, Mom. It's your last night here. I kind of like having him nearby."

Margaret scoffed. "I know how this little one sleeps, like a monkey trying to tear out of his cage. I heard you scold him for kicking you in the face last night when he worked his way to the end of the bed. Besides, he's totally out, so he won't know who's in bed with him."

"Really, Mom, I don't mind."

Rio started toward his room with Joseph still securely in his arms until Margaret said, "Wait a minute, Rio."

He turned back to mother and daughter, wishing they would make up their minds. He personally voted to have Joanna in his bed with him, if she should decide she needed company from someone other than her son. Not likely that was going to happen, but he could always hope.

Margaret brushed Joanna's hair away from her shoulders in an overt maternal gesture. "You look tired, Joanna. You'll have plenty of time to spend with him in the morning since our plane doesn't leave until late afternoon."

"But—"

"No buts. You need a good night's sleep or you'll be no good to anyone in the morning."

Looking somewhat defeated, Joanna sighed. "Okay, if you insist. But I'm warning you, he'll probably give you a few bruises."

Without waiting to see if the arrangements changed again, Rio scaled the steep stairs leading to the attic room, holding Joseph fast against his chest. Once inside, he laid him on the turned-down bed then slipped the sheet over him.

Rio, Joanna and Margaret stood and stared at the boy as if awaiting something momentous to occur. As far as Rio was concerned, that moment was fundamentally special, watching a child sleep, something he'd never before experienced beyond dozing newborns.

He didn't try to fight the unanticipated emotions streaming through him. He simply chalked it up to exhaustion even though it felt a lot like longing.

"Good night, you two," Margaret whispered, followed by a yawn. "Enjoy the rest of your evening together."

While Joanna looked stunned, Rio accepted the cue and walked out the door. Joanna kept her distance behind him and as they took the stairs, silence pervaded until they reached the second floor. Instead of leaving her in the hallway, Rio followed Joanna to her room—

his room, he corrected. A room with a king-size bed that could more than accommodate two people. He wanted to join Joanna there, to take her on an all-night journey into oblivion. After all, Margaret had practically given them permission.

Joanna obviously didn't see it that way, considering she glared at him from the open door. Even though she now wore a frown and that god-awful robe, Rio felt surprisingly energized, especially when he imagined untying the sash—with his teeth.

"Did you have fun today?" she asked with only a hint of amusement.

"I had a great time. And you have a great kid."

"I have to agree with you on that. I hope he didn't drive you totally crazy."

"Not at all. I can't remember when I've had such a good time." Rio sent a pointed look toward the master bath across the room behind her. "Actually, I do remember. Yesterday morning, in fact—"

Joanna clamped a hand over his mouth. "I don't think it's a good idea to discuss this now. Sound travels through the vents and I don't want my mom to accidentally overhear about…you know."

When Rio streaked his tongue across her palm, she dropped her hand from his mouth as if he'd burned her. "Maybe we should take this conversation into the bedroom and discuss…you know."

Joanna's eyes sparked with the desire he'd seen last night in the garage, the other morning in the bathroom, a few days ago in the hot tub, and with those memories came a stirring low in his gut. He was hard as hell and he wanted to do something about it. Now. But not unless she made the suggestion.

She gave him a semi-dirty look. "If you'll recall, I've

told you we need to avoid that kind of contact. Which reminds me. What was all that touching about today?"

Rio decided playing innocent might work best. "Are you referring to me holding your hand?"

"I'm referring to you trying to cop a feel underneath the restaurant table."

"I had my hand on your leg. If I'd tried something else, trust me, *querida,* you would have known the difference."

Rio detected a slight tremor in Joanna's body although they weren't close enough for him to be certain. He wished they were that close.

"Okay, so maybe you only rested your hand on my leg," she said. "But it was a little suggestive, don't you think?"

He braced his palm on the door frame above her head and leaned into her. "What do you suggest I was suggesting?"

"I don't know… I mean…you know."

Rio decided it would be incredibly easy to kiss her, lead her backward into the bedroom, right into his bed. Take off that robe again, get out of his jeans that were less than comfortable at the moment, and get down to the business of lovemaking. Slow, unrestrained, in the way that she deserved to be made love to.

Just when he considered delivering a convincing kiss, Joanna backed into the room and pointed to the opposite end of the hall. "Go to bed, Rio."

He pushed away from the door. "That's what I'm trying to do." Damn, why couldn't he hold up his end of the bargain? What had happened to her making the next move? Why did he find it so hard to keep his hands off her? His mind off her?

She looked as though she was asking herself those

same questions and didn't particularly like the answers. "You said you were going to wait until I came to you, did you not?"

"True."

"So go to bed before I..."

"Before you what?"

A grin crept in and lit up her crystalline eyes. "Before I change my mind and pull you down on the hall floor to do some horizontal Olympics." With that, she shut the door in his face.

Rio acknowledged it was going to be one helluva hard night. And when the time came, he was going to have one helluva hard time letting her go.

Nine

"I really like Rio, Joanna."

Joanna glanced up from the Sunday paper to find Margaret assessing her from across the dinette. First her son, now her mother. Rio had become very popular. "He's a nice man."

"And obviously very successful. Have you seen that marvelous game room?"

"Yes, I've seen it." She'd almost initiated the pool table with Rio, not that she would make that revelation to her mother.

"Joseph's in there now. Kid heaven, I tell you. So many toys, so little time."

Realizing Margaret was gearing up for a talk, Joanna folded the paper, tossed it aside and took a sip of coffee. "Rio's into toys. At times I think he's still very much a little boy."

Margaret frowned. "Maybe he's a bit carefree, but he

seems very responsible. I mean, he's a doctor. You should know better than anyone the kind of responsibility and commitment that requires."

Committed to his job, yes, Joanna acquiesced. But when it involved his personal life, he was committed only to his freedom. "Is there a point to this conversation, Mom?"

"Actually, I've been wondering if there's something going on between you two. Maybe a little more than meets the eye?"

Joanna fought a sudden surge of panic. "Why would you ask that?"

"Because yesterday he kept giving you *that* look."

"What look?"

"The same one your father used to give me when we were dating." Her smile was bittersweet. "The same one he gave me the whole time we were married."

"Look, Mom, Rio's just not that kind of guy. He's a great doctor and a good friend." A fantastic lover.

"And rather handsome, if you can get past the earring."

"But he's not the forever type."

"How do you know?"

Because he had made that quite clear to Joanna on more than one occasion. "Trust me, I just know."

"Men can change, Joanna."

"Adam never did."

Margaret frowned. "So that's it? You're comparing every man to Adam? You'll never be happy with anyone if you keep doing that."

Joanna turned the spoon resting near her hand over and over. "Maybe I don't need anyone other than my son, at least not another man."

"But Joseph does."

Joanna inwardly flinched at the truth in her mother's declaration. It had been all too apparent during the conversation two nights ago that Joseph had been thinking about having a father, and also how much he had enjoyed Rio's company. That worried her. "Rio's not a good candidate."

"Oh, I think he'd make a wonderful father for Joseph."

"Mother, please."

Margaret reached across the table, yanked the spoon from Joanna's grasp and took both Joanna's hands into her own. "Life has a way of surprising you, and so do some people if you give them a chance. Don't close yourself off to the possibilities or you'll end up like your father's sister, May. She was a bitter, vindictive old woman who delighted in making others suffer because she refused to open herself up to love once the preacher dumped her."

Joanna smiled at the memory of her aunt whom she'd greatly feared as a child and the legendary story of Aunt May's unrequited love. "I'll try not to turn into a shrew."

Margaret studied her with a mother's smile "Just remember, Joanna, dear. Sometimes you have to take that leap of faith and risk the fall in order to learn to live again."

Joanna refused to take the leap. She didn't dare hope that Rio would change his mind about commitment, or change at all for that matter. In reality, she wouldn't change anything about him. In fact, she loved most everything about him—his smile, his compassion, his innate wisdom, his free spirit. She loved…

Him?

Joanna didn't plan to go there. She didn't dare fall in

love with a man who had the hands of a healer and the heart of a renegade. But she feared she already had.

Rio stood back as Joanna said goodbye to her son and mother in the airport waiting area. He didn't care for goodbye scenes, especially this one, knowing how much Joanna was hurting. He could see it in the unshed tears brimming in her blue eyes when Joseph clung to her and begged to stay.

"I can sleep in the room by myself," Joseph said. "Like I do at Gran's. Gabby can sleep with me."

Joanna crouched on Joseph's level and braced his shoulders with her palms. "Honey, I promise it will only be a little while longer before you come to live with me again, right after you're out of school for the summer. I'll have a place for us to live then, a nice apartment with a swimming pool. Would you like that?"

Joseph stuck out his lip in a pout. "I don't want an old apartment. I want to live with Rio and Gabby. Besides, Rio has a pool. A big pool. And a bunch of games."

"Joseph, I'm only living with Dr. Madrid until I can find something else."

"But you said you liked him."

"Of course I like him, but I can't live with him forever."

Rio couldn't deny the twinge of bone-deep hurt over the prospect of Joanna leaving. He wanted to ignore the pain, shove it aside, but it kept jabbing at his insides, specifically in the vicinity of his heart. He just didn't know what the hell to do about it, not when she was so dead set against staying with him. And he wanted her to stay. God, did he want that. He hadn't realized how much until now. But he couldn't force her to make that decision.

The grating sound of the ticket agent announcing the call for boarding caused Joanna to straighten. Rio approached the threesome and held out his hand to Joseph. "You're welcome to come see me anytime, bud," he said in earnest.

Joseph ignored Rio's extended hand and opted to throw his arms around Rio's waist in a voracious hug. Giving in to a need he didn't understand and didn't want to claim, Rio picked Joseph up and held him tightly.

Joseph studied him with eyes much like his mother's, only they contained a definite trust that had been absent from Joanna's when she looked at Rio. "Did you save our last racing game on the video machine?"

Rio grinned. "Yeah, I saved it so we can take up where we left off, with you kicking my behind all over the virtual track."

"It's time to go, honey," Joanna said when the attendant made a last call to board.

Joseph reluctantly let go of Rio's neck, but not before giving him another hug. "Later, Rio."

"Later." Rio relinquished Joseph to his mother and turned his attention to Margaret. "Mrs. Mathis, it's been a pleasure."

She laid a hand on her throat and blushed. "Oh, stop it with the Mrs. I'm just Margaret, plain and simple." As her grandson had, she drew Rio into an embrace then whispered, "Take care of our girl, will you? Just don't let on that you are."

Rio pulled away and acknowledged her request with a simple nod though he doubted he would have that luxury.

Grandmother and grandson handed off their tickets

and started toward the jet way while Rio and Joanna looked on. Operating solely on instinct, he came up behind Joanna and pulled her into his arms, her back to his chest. She leaned heavily against him, as if her legs might give way while they watched the pair disappear.

In that moment, he wanted to take care of her. He wanted to give her all that she desired. He wanted to be the man she needed, but the honest truth stared him in the face as she pushed out of his arms and walked away.

The question no longer existed if he was willing to make a go of a real relationship, because he was. The problem now involved Joanna. She was doing her damnedest not to need anybody. Especially not him.

Joanna needed Rio more than anything at the moment. Her bed was too lonely and so was her heart. Having Joseph and her mother with her over the past two days had only cemented her loneliness now that they had left.

Unfortunately, Rio had left, too, immediately following their dinner. Retired to the garage, or so he'd told her. Other than that announcement, he'd been relatively quiet throughout the meal although several times he'd looked as if he'd wanted to say something.

She needed to tell him a few things as well. Explain why she couldn't stay much longer. If she remained in his home, in his life, she would only become more emotionally entangled. How could she subject her son to the possibility of getting too close to a man who had no designs on having a permanent relationship? How could she subject herself to that very thing?

At the moment, she didn't want to think about that. She wanted Rio to fill the void in her soul, right or wrong. She craved his company, craved his touch, so much so that she decided to seek him out, to be with him, if only one more time. She would make a few memories to take with her when she did decide to leave, hopefully with some of her heart intact.

Joanna left the solitude of her bedroom and padded down the stairs wearing a plain cotton gown covered by an all-weather coat, intending to start her search in the garage. When she caught the faint scent of wood smoke in the second-floor hallway, she walked to his bedroom and pushed open the door.

Other than a fire burning in the small hearth, the room was dark, deserted and she wondered if maybe Rio was still in the garage after all. Then she noted the sound of the shower running full force in the adjacent bathroom. Knowing he was in there, without a stitch of clothes, brought about a solid round of chills playing over Joanna's entire body, coupled with an overwhelming heat. She considered joining him in the shower but when she heard the water shut off, she realized it was too late.

No matter. She would wait for him in the bedroom. He'd wanted her to come to him, and that's exactly what she intended to do—come to him. Give herself to him, at least in a physical sense. She would be wise to leave it only at that, leave all the fuzzy feelings out of it. But the driving need to have him in her arms once more outweighed the risk to her emotions. That alone convinced her to continue as planned.

Joanna slipped off her coat and tossed it onto the small sofa in the sitting area. Perching on the edge of the bed closest to the bathroom, she made the snap decision to remove her gown and panties, leaving no room for doubt what she expected from Rio tonight. If she couldn't have forever, then she would settle for what she could have in the time that remained.

Naked and flushed, Joanna turned back the covers and

slipped beneath the cool black satin sheets. Tonight the smooth texture against her skin and Rio's lingering scent served to heighten her desire. Feeling brave and bold, she opted to cover herself only from the waist down, leaving her breasts exposed to his eyes when he came into the room.

For a few moments she wasn't sure if he would return, a ridiculous thought. Where else would he go? Out the bathroom window? Of course not. Silly, silly girl, she silently admonished. At least she wasn't quite as nervous as she had been when she'd come into the room—until the bathroom door opened.

Joanna closed her eyes and grabbed the sheet to cover herself. Maybe she wasn't so hot at seduction after all. But she was definitely hot. Extremely hot, especially when she opened her eyes to Rio standing next to the bed wearing nothing but a veiled expression.

"Are you lost, or did you miss my bed?" he asked, his voice as soft as a caress, deadly to her senses.

She rolled to one side and allowed the sheet to slide down, baring her breasts. "I've missed you." *I'm lost to you.*

He didn't move at all or respond, at least not with words. But because he was standing there in the altogether, he couldn't hide his body's reaction to her spontaneous seduction.

"I'm thinking you might have missed me a little, too," she said with a pointed look below his tattoo at proof positive she'd gotten his attention.

"What do you want, Joanna?"

"I want you."

"Are you sure it's me you want? Or maybe you just need a little comfort. Something to get your mind off the fact you had to tell your son goodbye."

She logically couldn't deny any of that, yet seeing Joseph and her mother off was only part of the reason. "I need to be with you, Rio. I *want* to be with you. You've told me I had to make the next move, so I'm making it."

A muscle twitched in his jaw, his only movement. "You better be certain, Joanna, because if I get into that bed with you, I'm going to make sure that you don't have the will to change your mind."

"And how do you intend to do that?"

"With my hands, with my mouth. And everything in between."

Joanna drew in a deep breath and tossed the sheet away. "I don't plan to change my mind."

His eyes darkened and his hands opened and closed at his sides. For the longest moment she thought he was going to refuse her until he moved closer to the bed. Then he abruptly turned and headed back into the bathroom.

Joanna's heart sank to her heels and she felt like screaming from frustration. Then he reentered the room and tossed two condoms onto the bedside table. Her heart took flight and now she felt like shouting from relief.

He slid onto the bed but instead of taking her into his arms, he took her hands and pulled her up until they sat opposite each other on their knees, face-to-face, covered only in the illumination coming from the hearth.

In that moment, Rio became the fire, from the golden glow of his eyes to the heat radiating from his body. And like the proverbial moth, Joanna was drawn to the flame.

He continued to study her a few moments until he finally said, "Convince me."

Hadn't she done that by coming to his room and stripping? "I beg your pardon?"

"Convince me that you want this."

Joanna knew of only one way to do that. She raised a trembling hand to his chest over the place where his heart beat strong and steady. Sliding her palm over his taut damp skin, she began her journey by tracing a path with one fingertip from the spattering of dark hair down along the ribbon to his navel. She paused at the tattoo to explore the territory the way she had wanted to the night she'd first seen it. The image was muted in the limited light but Joanna could still experience its power, as well as the power she had over Rio at the moment when his muscles constricted beneath her hand. She reveled in that dominance and wanted more of it, more of him. All of him.

As she inched lower, Joanna watched his face for his reaction. His expression remained almost detached, as solid as stone, until she took matters completely into her hands. His eyes narrowed and his chest rose with a sharp intake of breath when she caressed him, learned the differing textures with curious fingers. His flesh was hot, rigid and totally tempting, bringing her to the verge of complete meltdown. That didn't stop her from studying the length and breadth of him—until Rio's hand circled her wrist, halting her exploration.

"I'm convinced."

Joanna sent him a sinister grin. "But I'm not quite done."

"Yeah, you are."

"No, I'm not." Before he could deliver another protest, Joanna lowered her head and took him into her mouth. She felt the change in him immediately as his fingers entwined in her hair. Yet he only allowed her the pleasure for a moment before he stopped her by pulling her head up to deliver an earth-tilting kiss.

Yet the kiss didn't last long before he broke the contact. Then, as she had, he conducted his own expedition over her body with a fervent touch that left her winded and hot and aching. He fondled her breasts, graced her nipples with soft, circular movements, ran his thumbs along her sides, slipped his hand between her thighs to touch her with a gentle yet insistent sweep of his fingertips, bringing her close to a climax. But right before she shattered, he took his hand away.

Joanna released a groan of protest that brought about Rio's own devilish smile. "Do you want more?"

"Yes," she said in a pleading tone.

"How much more?"

"Everything, dammit."

He nipped at her bottom lip and soothed it with his tongue. "I like it when you're tough. It excites me."

She kissed his left ear and flicked the gold loop with her tongue. "When I want something badly enough, I've been known to drive a hard bargain."

He held her hand against his erection. "So do I."

"Convince me," she said, throwing his own words back at him.

"My pleasure."

Rio nudged her onto her back then fumbled for a condom from the nightstand. As he sheathed himself, Joanna clawed his back, desperate to have him immediately. He responded by holding her hands at bay over her head as he uttered one harsh oath in English, a word that Joanna had no trouble understanding. Slang for the act, crude in any language, yet it sent potent shudders down Joanna's spine to think that she had driven him to the sudden loss of control. But his lack of control was short-lived as he entered her in a slow, steady glide then pulled away until she lifted her hips to urge him into her needy body.

The mood quickly changed from fast and furious to slow and sultry when Rio continued in an easy rhythm, allowing Joanna to take the moments to memory, to absorb the sensations as he buried his face in her neck and whispered wonderful endearments. When he finally released her hands, she stroked his damp, silky hair, breathed in his scent, savored the feel of him so intimately connected to her.

In those quiet moments, she realized they were making love, at least she was, because despite her determination not to love him, she did. With all of her wounded heart, she loved him. And for a split second as he held her securely against his heart, she allowed herself to imagine that he loved her too.

With gentle, questing fingertips, he touched her above the place where they were joined, bringing her to another astounding climax while he moved inside her. A keening sound crept up her throat and slipped between her parted lips. Never before had she known such incredible pleasure. Never before had she felt so close to coming apart, so close to feeling wholly joined to another's soul, so hopelessly lost to a man who had completely captivated her, body, heart and soul.

''Do you know what you're doing to me, *mi amante?*'' Rio said in a strained voice as he battled to hold on a little longer. ''Do you know how incredible you feel?''

Joanna answered with another tilt of her hips to take him deeper inside. The movement drove his body to make demands he couldn't disregard. He surrendered with a wilder, more reckless tempo, bringing on a climax that arrived with the force of an explosion, making him shake from the power of the release. Making him feel things he'd never felt before.

He drifted back to consciousness in slow increments, well aware that something phenomenal had happened again, and it still had little to do with sex. The woman in his arms, joined to his body, had totally worked her way beneath his skin, invaded his soul, claimed his heart.

Joanna shifted and although he didn't want to let her go, he tried to move enough to lessen his weight.

''Don't leave,'' she said. ''I want to remember this.''

Rio would never forget this moment, this act, this woman, and he couldn't seem to get close enough to her. The connection to Joanna went beyond the bounds of their physical union, as if everything suddenly made sense.

When Rio rolled to his back, taking her with him, Joanna nestled her warm cheek against his shoulder and sighed.

Rio stroked the dip at her spine and lingered there. The prospect of sending his hand lower to explore made his body stir once more. No doubt, he wanted to make love to her again—and again—as soon as he'd had enough time to recover. First, he needed to say something, and he began with an idea that had come to him earlier in the day. ''I've been thinking.''

Joanna brushed a tender kiss across his neck. ''About what?''

''About this summer. I was thinking maybe we could take a couple of months off and travel the country. You, me and Joseph, and your mom if you'd like.''

Joanna tensed in his arms. ''I can't just take off, Rio. I have responsibilities and debts. A good job, and so do you.''

"My job will be here when we return. I'll pay your debts."

"In exchange for what?"

"To keep you here. We can fix up a room for Joseph and one for your mother if she wants to come and stay for a while."

She moved onto her back, breaking the intimate contact, raising an intangible wall. "That's not possible. Joseph is already too enamored of you. I don't want him to think that this arrangement is permanent."

Anger threatened Rio's euphoric mood. "Arrangement?"

"Our living together."

An illogical stab of desperation impaled him. "Are you saying that you're not willing to see if this will work out between us?"

"What happened to no ties, no commitment?"

"I don't know. Being around you and Joseph this weekend made me realize that something's been missing from my life."

She sighed. "That was only two days, Rio. Are you really being honest with yourself? Are you really willing to commit to more than an occasional weekend?"

"I'm willing to try, Joanna. See where it goes from here."

"Call me old-fashioned, but I can't just live with you, especially with Joseph under the same roof."

"I don't know what you want from me."

She sat up and ran a hand through her tangled hair. "I don't want anything from you, Rio. Not beyond what happened tonight. I know how much you enjoy your freedom except when it comes to your work. But I guess I was wrong about that, too."

"Why? Because I want to take some time off?"

"Because it seems so easy for you to leave everything behind. I'm worried you'll eventually do the same to us. I don't want to get left behind again, and I definitely don't want that for my son. It scares me to think that might happen."

Rio pushed himself up and leaned back against the headboard. "You think this is easy for me? I've never had a real relationship with a woman, Joanna. I've never wanted one until now. You're responsible for that. You've changed me."

She leveled her gaze on him. "I'd love to believe that but I'm afraid I've heard it all before."

"I'm not your ex-husband. I have more honor than that."

She clutched the comforter to her breasts as if the intimacy between them was too much to bear. "You are an honorable man, Rio. I know that better than anyone, and that's one of the things I love about you."

Rio wasn't sure he'd heard correctly. "What did you say?"

"I said I love you, and I do. Believe me, that's the last thing I wanted, but I can't help the way I feel."

"If that's true, then why not stay with me?"

"I'm afraid that you won't be satisfied with some mundane existence, and I can't stay knowing we're not completely committed to each other."

"Are you talking about marriage?" The word tasted bitter, sounded harsh, brought back recollections of his mother's less-than-happy union with his stepfather. "I've never understood why having a piece of paper is so important if two people really care about each other. And I do care about you."

Tossing back the covers, Joanna came to her feet and retrieved her gown from the end of the bed. She slipped it on in silence then said, "You're right. Marriage is the last thing that either one of us needs. Good night, Rio."

Her good-night sounded a lot like goodbye to Rio. Before she could leave the room, he bolted from the bed, clasped her arm and turned her around. "Stay with me, Joanna."

"We both need to get some sleep."

He took a chance and pulled her against him. "Not only tonight. Stay with me beyond the summer."

Even in the muted light, he could see the indecision in her eyes as well as a trace of pain. "I have to do what's best for me, Rio. For my son. Please understand."

After she walked away, Rio took his fury out on the dying fire, grabbing up the poker and jabbing what was left of the logs. He'd known all along what Joanna needed, someone she could trust to stay by her side, through thick and thin. She also needed to hear the words that he'd been too much of a coward to say—that he loved her, too, and he was beginning to believe he did love her. More than he could express.

He also recognized that he needed to convince Joanna that he intended to be there for her and Joseph whether they had a license or not. To convince her that once he made a commitment, he would stick to it, the same as he had with his goals to become a doctor.

Rio had a lot to consider, and not much time left at all. Deep in his soul, he knew that Joanna would be gone long before the arrival of summer, unless he persuaded her to stay. If only he knew how to do that.

Ten

The following afternoon at his office, Rio received a message from Joanna asking him to meet her at the hospital. Allison Cartwright was in trouble.

Minutes later, Rio rushed out of the elevator and onto the labor and delivery floor, practically running into Joanna head-on. She looked worried and tired but he didn't have time to dwell on anything but Allison's complications.

"Where is she?" he asked.

Joanna pointed toward the corridor. "In 502. She's got an elevated pressure and she's dumping protein in her urine."

"She's preeclamptic," Rio stated with certainty.

"Looks like it, but her pressure was only slightly outside the norm when I saw her last week. I put her on bed rest but it hasn't helped. That's why I brought her here."

''You did the right thing,'' he assured her. ''She's what, about thirty-five weeks gestation?''

''Thirty-six.''

''Then the baby's viable, so induction is probably the best option. Do you agree?''

Joanna frowned. ''Of course, but it's your decision since she's your patient.''

''She's *our* patient, and I want you with me.'' Today. Next week. Forever.

The thoughts vaulted into Rio's brain, sharp as a switchblade, but now wasn't the time to discuss what he wanted from Joanna. Later, he decided. He'd tell her later, after they took care of Allison.

''I'll be with you every step of the way, at least through Allison's labor,'' Joanna said. There was a finality to her words, and Rio fought an odd panic that she was already planning to leave, that he was already too late.

Rio turned away from her and strode down the hallway before he gave in to the urge to pull her into his arms. Before he told her all the things that had haunted him through the night as well as today, things he should have told her last night. He didn't have time to make any revelations. He couldn't be the man when he was expected to be the doctor.

Joanna followed him into Allison's room where Rio forced himself into medical mode, immediately noting the fear in Allison's expression.

''Hey, Allison,'' he said in his well-practiced calm voice despite his growing concern.

She drew in a long breath and released it slowly. ''Hi, Dr. Madrid. Glad you could join us for the party.'' Her attempt at wry humor didn't mask her anxiety.

Rio walked to the head of the bed and studied the tape

spilling from the monitor that registered the baby's heartbeat. Thank God everything looked fine in that department. Unfortunately, Allison's blood pressure didn't. "I guess Joanna told you about your preeclampsia."

Allison nodded. "Yes, and what do we do now?"

Rio hid his apprehension behind a smile. "In light of your condition, Joanna and I have decided we need to go ahead and induce your labor and watch you carefully."

Allison turned frightened eyes to him and then to Joanna. "But I still have a month to go."

"The risk to you and the baby will increase if you don't deliver now," Joanna said. "This is for the best."

Tears drifted down Allison's cheeks and she quickly swiped them away with one trembling hand. "Okay, then. If there aren't any other options, then I guess I'll have a baby."

Joanna offered a gentle smile aimed at Allison but it impacted Rio clear down to his soul. He couldn't imagine not seeing that smile on a daily basis. Seeing her on a daily basis.

"It's going to be okay, Allison," Joanna said. "We'll have the neonatology team standing by."

Allison tipped her chin up in a show of bravado. "Then let's get this show on the road. I'm ready."

After Rio ordered the meds to begin Allison's labor, a passing nurse stuck her head in the door and announced that he had an unexpected admit nearing delivery.

"I'll stay here," Joanna said when the nurse departed. "You go ahead and take care of your other patient. I'm sure you'll be back in plenty of time."

Rio was reluctant to leave but recognized that Joanna was more than capable of handling the situation until his return. ''Okay, but keep me informed. If anything happens, page me—''

''I will. I promise.''

As it turned out, by the time Rio's patient delivered and he completed his afternoon rounds, four hours had passed before he made it back to Allison's room.

Joanna greeted him immediately outside the door. ''It's happening fast,'' she said. ''Her water broke and she's completely dilated. She's been pushing for a while now. The charge nurse, Sara Gilmore, is going to assist.''

At least that was good news. ''Why didn't you page me?''

''It wasn't necessary. I knew you'd be back soon.''

Rio ran a hand over his scalp. ''Her pressure?''

''Still high but not in the danger zone. Yet.''

''We both know that the only cure for preeclampsia is delivering the baby, so let's get going.''

Joanna stopped him by clasping his arm. ''I just wanted to thank you, Rio.''

''What for?''

She looked at him with her heart in her eyes. ''For trusting me.''

He wanted to ask her to trust him, trust that he would do right by her but instead he said, ''You're a great midwife, Joanna.'' An extraordinary mother. An incredible lover. A fantastic friend. ''You'd make a great doctor.''

She grinned. ''You think so?''

His smile surfaced in response. ''I know so. Now let's go deliver a baby. Together.'' As if everything was okay between them, he couldn't resist giving her a playful swat on the bottom as she entered the room.

All playfulness disappeared when Sara reported, ''Her

pressure's at 160/110. The good news is the baby's head is starting to crown.''

As Rio viewed Allison's pale, sweat-drenched face and the monitor that revealed her pressure hovering in a precariously high range, he was abruptly thrust back to another time, another place with another young woman he hadn't been able to save. For a brief moment, he became the teenage boy once more, the one who had been inadequate, helpless to do anything but stand by and watch a young mother die.

He reminded himself that he wasn't that boy. He was a doctor. He had acquired knowledge and skills. Although he recognized some situations were out of his control, he'd be damned if he'd let anything happen to Allison Cartwright or her baby. Better still, he had Joanna on his side and that alone provided him with much-needed determination.

Forcing himself into action, Rio barked an order for magnesium sulfate to prevent the possibility of seizures. ''Allison, Sara's going to give you some medicine in your IV so we don't have any additional problems. You might feel flushed and drowsy, but that's normal.''

''The baby?'' Allison croaked, followed by a strained breath.

''You're almost there but we're going to need your help.''

The door opened and neonatologist Brendan O'Connor walked in with a nurse pushing a portable warmer trailing behind him.

''Just in time, Dr. O'Connor,'' Joanna said.

''Good to see you again, Brendan,'' Rio added.

''Same here.'' Brendan approached Allison. ''Ms. Cartwright, I'm Dr. O'Connor, the neonatologist on duty. I'll be taking care of your baby as a precaution.

Considering you're relatively close to term, hopefully your baby won't be needing my services long term."

"I hope so…too." Allison grimaced and cried, "Here it comes…again!"

Rio took his place at the end of the bed with Joanna as Brendan stood to one side to await the baby's arrival. While Joanna and Sara offered encouragement, Rio asked Allison to push again.

Allison collapsed against the bed before any progress had been made and Rio realized that her strength was waning. "I know you're tired, Allison, but I need a little more from you."

"I'm trying," she said, followed by a sob. "But I don't have anything left."

"Come on, Allison," Joanna coaxed. "You can't give up now."

Rio glanced at the monitor, checking Allison's vitals and realizing all too well that time was of the essence. His options were limited if Allison wasn't able to cooperate and he had no choice but to be prepared for that instance. "Notify staff and tell them to ready for a C-section just in case," he said to Sara.

Allison showed amazing strength at that moment as she sat up and glared at him. "No C-section. I can do this."

"Okay," Rio said. "Give it all you've got."

Joanna urged Allison to bear down, harder this time. As Rio offered his own verbal prodding, he marveled at Joanna's unrelenting fortitude in the face of adversity. Together they worked as a team, totally in sync, completely in tune with each other. Allison finally gave one more push, allowing Rio to deliver the baby's head.

Joanna gave Rio a thumbs-up and Rio gave the order for one more gentle push from Allison.

Finally, the child slid completely into Rio's waiting hands. ''You've got a girl, Allison,'' he said as the baby let loose a resounding cry. ''A beautiful baby girl.''

As Rio cradled the infant in one arm, it occurred to him how at times he had taken this process for granted. But with Joanna by his side, he saw a glimpse of the future, the possibility that maybe one day he would be a father holding his own child. His and Joanna's child.

He clamped the cord and held it up. ''Joanna, will you do the honors?''

With a satisfied expression, Joanna complied. Rio handed the baby off to Brendan O'Connor, relieved that the infant's color looked good.

''Is she okay?'' Allison asked in a tear-filled voice.

Brendan spoke without turning from the newborn. ''She looks great so far and she's breathing on her own, but I need to take her to the NICU and observe her for at least twenty-four hours.''

''Can I see her first?'' Allison asked.

''Sure.'' Brendan placed the baby in her mother's arms and stepped away from the bed.

Rio noticed that the exhaustion on Allison's face disappeared with the first glimpse of her daughter. ''You were supposed to be a boy, little one.'' She brushed a kiss across the baby's cheek. ''But you're still my miracle.''

As far as Rio was concerned, every birth, every baby was indeed a miracle, and so was the fact that he had found Joanna. He wanted to tell her right then, but he didn't want an audience playing witness when he spilled his guts.

After he finished his final doctor duties and the baby had been whisked away in the care of Brendan O'Connor, Rio looked up to see Allison reclined on the bed, her eyes closed against the fluorescent lights. He searched the room for Joanna only to discover she was missing. That sure as hell wouldn't do. He had to find her and fast, before he lost his nerve. Before another minute passed when he could say what was on his mind, in his heart.

Quietly he turned to leave Allison in Sara's care until "Dr. Madrid" came from behind him.

He faced the bed to find Allison now looking wide awake. "I thought you were asleep," he said.

"I'm not sure how much I'll be able to sleep until I know the baby's okay."

"You need to try and rest. Once you have her home, sleep might be at a premium."

"Since I doubt I still have a job, I'll have plenty of time for that."

Rio moved back to her side and sent her a sympathetic look. "Is there anyone I can call for you?"

She shook her head. "I'll phone my dad in a while, but he's in New Jersey with my sister."

"Anyone else that might want to know?" Rio realized he was fishing, but he hated to see Allison go through this alone.

She turned away from him and focused on the window but not before he saw a few latent tears. "No."

"Okay. Just let me know if you change your mind."

Allison met his gaze. "Thanks for everything. And you know something? You two were amazing."

"Excuse me?"

"You and Joanna. The way you both worked together to deliver my baby was absolutely incredible, as if you were practically one person. Most people live all their lives hoping for that kind of synchronicity in a relationship."

He had hoped for the same though he'd never realized it until now. Until Joanna. "We work well together."

Allison afforded him a grin. "It goes way beyond your working relationship. Anyone with half a brain can tell that you two love each other."

He shot a glance in Sara's direction. She appeared to be paying more attention to the cleanup than the conversation, but Rio knew better. "Get some sleep," he said to Allison in a mock-firm tone to cover his sudden self-consciousness.

"I promise I'll try. As long as you promise to hang on to what you and Joanna have found together."

Exactly what Rio had planned. "I'll see what I can do. Wish me luck."

"Good luck," Sara said, her back turned to him and a smile in her voice.

"You don't need any luck," Allison said. "Not as long as you have each other."

If he could just be assured that he would have Joanna. Only one way to find out.

After Rio told Allison and Sara goodbye, a deep-seated longing followed him all the way down the hall while determination quickened his steps in his search for Joanna.

She was very much a part of him now, as his mother had told him it would be with the special woman destined to change his life. He hadn't believed her, hadn't believed that he would ever be capable of loving someone as much as he loved Joanna, or that he would hurt so badly over the prospect of losing her.

To hell with his old ideas about marriage. He wasn't his stepfather, and she wasn't his mother. Commitment was no longer an unpalatable prospect. He valued all that

Joanna was as a person, valued her love, and if he had to get a license to prove it, then so be it.

Rio experienced a sudden sense of liberation as he acknowledged that he had finally found true freedom through his love for Joanna Blake.

Now if he could only find her.

Joanna entered the NICU to check on Allison's daughter and came upon Brendan O'Connor talking to a respiratory therapist. She hung back until the conversation ended before addressing the neonatologist. "Hi again."

His drop-dead smile and calm demeanor left no room for doubt in Joanna's mind as to why Cassie had fallen for this particular physician. "Hey, Joanna. Great work during the Cartwright delivery. Maybe Cassie and I should consider hiring you and Dr. Madrid with our next baby."

"I'll keep that in mind over the next couple of years."

He glanced away. "Try the next seven months."

Joanna's eyes widened. "Cassie's pregnant again?"

Brendan's chagrin turned into a self-satisfied smile. "Yeah, she is. We didn't exactly expect it to be quite this soon, but Cassie's always said that the best things in life aren't planned, and I couldn't agree more."

Neither could Joanna. She certainly hadn't planned to encounter a devastating doctor on New Year's Eve, but she had, and regardless that she saw no real future for them, she would never regret meeting—or loving—Rio Madrid.

"Congratulations, Brendan. I think it's wonderful. Tell Cassie I'll call her soon."

"I'm sure she'd appreciate some adult conversation."

Joanna decided she might need Cassie's shoulder to

cry on in the near future. She scanned the rows of cribs, most housing critically ill infants. ''Where's baby Cartwright?''

Brendan gestured across the large area divided into various sections according to the level of care. ''She's in intermediate at the back of the unit. She looks great. I'll probably release her in the next couple of days.''

''That's wonderful news, and if it's okay, I'd like to check on her before I leave.''

''No problem. But just so you know, she has another visitor at the moment.''

Joanna immediately considered that Rio had beaten her to the punch. ''Dr. Madrid's here?''

''No. Dr. Billings, the neurosurgeon.''

''Is a neuro check standard?''

''No, and he doesn't handle pediatrics. He just showed up all of a sudden and asked to see her. Beyond that, I have no idea why he's here.''

The cogs in Joanna's brain started turning at warp speed. ''Tell me something, Brendan. Is Dr. Billings married?''

''No. Why? Are you interested in him?''

Lord, no. She had more doctor than she could handle in Rio. ''Nope. Just curious.'' She started toward the rear of the room to avoid more questions. ''I'm going to see the baby.'' And to size up Dr. Lane Billings.

Maybe her imagination was running helter-skelter, but Joanna couldn't help wondering if the neurosurgeon might be the missing link in the Cartwright baby's parentage.

After stopping a resident who pointed out the newborn, Joanna hesitated in the aisle when she noticed the man standing over the transparent crib. She wouldn't have pegged him as a doctor had it not been for the lab coat covering his boot-cut cowboy jeans and the plastic credentials pinned to his lapel. His medium-brown hair looked as if he'd run his fingers through it several times, but aside from that, he had above-average looks. His tanned skin indicated he'd spent a lot of time out of doors. His sober expression revealed he very well could have suffered a recent shock. One that might involve learning he had a new daughter.

Feeling like an intruder, Joanna considered leaving him alone. Unanswered questions drove her forward.

She moved next to the doctor and looked down on the sleeping infant. "A beautiful baby, isn't she?"

Billings looked at her, surprise reflecting in his dark-brown eyes. "Yeah, she is."

Joanna offered her hand. "I'm Joanna Blake, the midwife who assisted in the delivery."

He took her hand into his for a brief shake. "Dr. Lane Billings."

"Nice to meet you. Are you here to check out the baby?"

"No."

"Just visiting then?"

"You could say that."

A man of few words, Joanna decided. Or perhaps he didn't appreciate her nosiness. "I take it you know Allison."

"She worked for me at one time."

"Really? I thought she worked for attorneys."

"Not until seven months ago. I've been gone a while. I only returned to Memorial about a month ago."

Joanna did a mental countdown. Seven months would be about right in terms of timing and Allison's pregnancy. And Allison had said that the baby's father had been on leave.

He turned his attention back to the infant. ''Is she okay?''

''Dr. O'Connor said she's doing great.''

''I meant Allison. O'Connor told me she had a rough delivery. Something about preeclampsia.''

''It was touch-and-go for a while but she's fine. She'll probably need to stay here a few extra days.'' Joanna took a breath and a chance. ''Since she has no family around here, I'm sure she'd love to see you.''

''I'm not sure she would.''

''Oh. Then you didn't part on good terms.''

He lowered his head. ''I didn't know she was pregnant. If I had known, I wouldn't have taken off like I did.''

The puzzle was finally coming together though Lane Billings looked as if he might come apart. ''Maybe you should tell her.''

He released a coarse, weary sigh. ''I'm not sure she'll believe me. I wouldn't blame her if she didn't.'' He met Joanna's gaze. ''I have no idea why I'm telling you all of this.''

''Me, neither, but Allison is my friend as well as my patient, and I think you should talk to her.''

''Maybe I will. At least I can try.''

Joanna nodded toward the infant who seemed totally serene among the clanks, bells and clatter of the NICU. ''You owe it to her.''

Billings's gaze returned to the little girl with the light-brown hair and a small cleft in her chin, a miniature mirror image of the doctor. ''I owe both of them. Life is too short to keep making the same mistakes over and over.''

How well Joanna knew that concept. And because she

did have that personal knowledge, she also knew what she had to do after she left the hospital.

Backing away from the crib, she murmured, ''Good luck,'' then turned and left the doctor, hoping that maybe somehow he and Allison could at least make amends, if not a family.

Joanna longed to have a family too. One that included Rio. But that wasn't going to be possible, not unless Rio was willing to cross the self-imposed boundaries that kept him from commitment. She also realized that with each passing day, it would only become more difficult to distance herself from him.

For that reason, she'd come to the conclusion that leaving Rio now would be best, before she couldn't leave him at all.

Eleven

Joanna gathered the last of her things and put them into the final box then surveyed the lilac room with yearning and sadness. She might miss this place, but she would definitely miss Rio more.

After leaving the hospital, she'd returned to the center and approached the administrator about temporarily staying in the on-call room. She'd received an affirmative answer but with the deal came the agreement that she would take call most of the time for the next four months. No problem for Joanna since she would need all her hours filled in order not to think about Rio or how much she missed her son.

In the meantime, Joanna would focus on the good things that had happened today. She'd received a great review, a substantial salary increase and with any luck at all, she would save enough money to pay off a few more bills, find a suitable place for her and Joseph to live by the time summer rolled around. It wouldn't be the same as living with Rio, but it was the best she could do for now.

Joanna made a mental note to call and check on Allison before she left the house, but first she intended to load her car. Gathering the box under one arm and draping her hanging clothes over the other, she trudged down both flights of stairs and stopped at the bottom to look up at the stained-glass cat that seemed to be staring at her with judgment.

"I have to go. I don't have a choice." Talking to an inanimate object made Joanna feel somewhat ridiculous, but her feelings of regret overrode all others. She didn't really want to go but she knew she must.

Although Joanna wanted to avoid a confrontation, leaving without Rio's knowledge seemed totally unfair. She decided to wait until he returned home. She owed him at least that much. She owed him a lot. He'd taken her into his home without question, welcomed her son with a kindness she'd rarely seen in Joseph's own father, and he'd made love to her as if she really mattered, even if he didn't love her in the way that she wanted to be loved.

The sound of hoof-paws echoed in the foyer as Gabby came bounding in. Amazingly, the dog rose up and planted her massive feet on Joanna's chest.

"A fine time for you to get sentimental on me, Gabby girl. Normally you wouldn't bother to give me the time of day. But then you probably just need some attention and I'm the only one available. Now get down for a sec and I'll pet you."

Gabby complied, her tail wagging furiously. Joanna set down her things, took a seat on the bottom step and gave the dog a good scratching behind her ears while she waited. Tears filled Joanna's eyes and Gabby stared at her with an almost sympathetic look, as if she knew how hard it was for Joanna to go.

"It'll be okay," Joanna said in a soft voice. "He'll be okay. After all, he has you. He doesn't really need me."

"Yes, he does."

Joanna's hand stopped midstroke on Gabby's coarse fur and her gaze drifted to the den's entry. And there stood Rio, his hands shoved in his jeans pockets, a black T-shirt drawn tightly over his chest, his dark hair pulled back at his nape to reveal the gold earring twinkling like the chandelier above them. Almost the picture-perfect image he had presented the night she'd left him in the ballroom, minus the suit and the smile.

Joanna's heart took a little tumble. Had she really heard him right? He needed her? Maybe so, but need and love were two entirely different things, so she had to remain strong.

He approached her and surveyed her with pensive eyes. "I've been looking all over for you at the hospital."

"I stopped by the NICU to see Allison's baby."

"So did I, but I must have just missed you."

"Must have."

He eyed her belongings set out on the stairs. "Are you going somewhere?"

Joanna stood on wobbly knees and all the emotions she had been determined to hold back welled up inside her. Her eyes blurred from the tears she didn't want to claim. "I can't stay, Rio. Not with the way things now stand between us."

He held out his hand. "Come with me upstairs. I want to show you something."

If he meant to persuade her by taking her to his bed, she'd never be able to leave. ''Rio, I really don't think—''

''Trust me, Joanna. This is important.'' His compelling voice, his solemn expression, drove her to take his hand.

As if she had no will of her own, Joanna allowed him to lead her back up the stairs, his grip firmly intertwined with hers, her heart soundly tangled up in her love for him. They entered his bedroom where he seated her on the small sofa facing the fireplace. The lingering smell of wood smoke blending with incense brought back memories of the night before when Rio had stoked the fire within her, a flame that still smoldered regardless of her attempts to douse it.

But Dr. Rio Madrid wasn't easy to ignore, even now when he crossed the room to the bureau near his bed. She concentrated on the roll of his narrow hips encased in faded denim, thinking he was such a dichotomy—sensual male interwoven with consummate doctor. Another thing she dearly loved about him.

He returned to her holding a small faded jade-colored box in one large palm. After taking a seat beside her, he opened the box to a silver ring with a topaz stone. ''This was my mother's,'' he said. ''My father gave it to her when they married. He bought it off of a street vendor in San Diego, supposedly with all the money he had.''

Joanna surveyed the ring and found it beautiful in its simplicity. ''That's a wonderful story.''

''Try it on.''

Joanna raised her gaze from the ring to his powerful golden eyes. Without waiting for her response, Rio pulled it from the box and slid it onto Joanna's left ring finger. ''It's perfect,'' he said. ''I knew it would be.''

Joanna couldn't fathom what was happening. Was he presenting her with a goodbye gift? A token of his esteem? Something to remember him by? As if she really needed an object as a reminder of him, of what they had shared. "I can't accept this, Rio. It has to have a lot of sentimental value."

He brought her hand to his lips and kissed her finger right above the ring. "It belongs to you, Joanna. Just as we belong together."

Joanna's heart shuffled into her throat. "I don't understand."

"Yes, you do. I'm saying I love you. I'm saying that I'm willing to make a commitment to you and Joseph, and I want to prove it."

Joanna was nearly rendered speechless. "By giving me a ring?"

"The ring is a token. I intend to give you more." He brushed a gentle kiss over her lips. "My mother once told me about a Mayan ceremony when lovers unite for life. I wasn't paying much attention to what was involved, so that means we'll have to go with the contemporary method, a license and someone official to perform the ceremony."

"Are you asking me—"

"To marry me. Yeah, I am." He sighed. "I realize how much your ex-husband hurt you, Joanna. I know you're probably scared about the whole marriage thing and honestly I'm scared, too, but I promise to do my best to make you happy."

Joanna wanted badly to say yes, but she still had a few unanswered questions. "I love being a midwife and I plan to continue doing it regardless of what happens between us."

He took both her hands into his. "Today, when we

worked together, I don't remember ever admiring anyone as much as I admired you. You're strong and smart and damn good at what you do."

"Then I've changed your mind about midwives?"

"My mother was a midwife. She provided services for indigent women who couldn't afford insurance. I used to attend the births with her when I was a teenager. For the most part, she did well by her patients until one night when a young woman in her care died while I stood by and watched, helpless to do anything to save her. My mother quit after that and I vowed that I would do everything in my power not to let something like that young woman's death happen again."

"That's what drove you to be an obstetrician?"

"Yeah. Despite that terrible night, my mother taught me many things and until I met you, I hadn't really understood her as well as I should have. She was a great lady."

Joanna was only beginning to understand the complex facets that made up Rio Madrid. That didn't matter. She had a lifetime to get to know them all. "Your mother raised a terrific son who happens to be an incredible, skilled doctor. A wonderful man who I'd be honored to have as my husband."

"Then you're saying—"

"Yes."

"What?"

Joanna's joy bubbled out in a laugh. "Yes, I'll marry you."

Rio framed her face in his palms. "Thank God. I thought you might tell me to go to hell." He stroked his thumbs back and forth over her cheeks. "I'll always be honest with you from this point forward, Joanna. I swear it."

She laid her palms over his hands. ‘‘I’ve come to realize that in order to trust you, I have to trust myself. Trust what I’m feeling. And right now I’m feeling fairly great.’’

Rio laughed then and Joanna reveled in the joyous sound. ‘‘I still can’t believe you said yes to a rogue like me.’’

Joanna’s own joy came through in a grin. ‘‘You know something, I would have said yes if you’d asked me last night. Heck, I probably would have said yes if you’d asked me that first night we kissed on New Year’s Eve.’’

His smile turned decidedly devilish. ‘‘I would have asked you for something else that night if you’d stuck around.’’

‘‘And what would that have been?’’

‘‘Maybe I should show you.’’ He kissed her then—a moving, emotional kiss that somehow turned passionate and provocative, leaving them both winded by the time they parted.

Pulling back, he worked the buttons on her plain cotton blouse, parted the fabric and palmed her lace-covered breast with one talented hand. Then suddenly he went motionless and rested his forehead against hers.

Joanna wrapped her arms around his neck. ‘‘You must be really scared. You’re shaking.’’

He raised his eyes to hers and Joanna finally saw it, an emotion she had never really seen before. Or maybe she’d been too afraid to notice it until now—too afraid that she might be mistaken. But it was there, a love as endless as his compassion, as strong as his magnetic gaze.

‘‘I’m shaking because I want you too much,’’ he finally said. ‘‘It’s been a long time.’’

‘‘It’s been less than twenty-four hours, Rio.’’

"Too long, in my opinion."

Scooping her up into his arms, Rio laid her on the bed and divested her of all remaining clothing, planting kisses on bare skin after the departure of each article. By the time he'd completely undressed, Joanna was on the verge of pleading for him to end the sensual torment. Before she could, he entered her with a leisurely glide and gave her a deep, meaningful kiss.

"I won't leave you, Joanna," he said as he moved in a measured tempo that prolonged the blessed agony.

"I know." And she did, with every beat of her heart.

Joanna held on to Rio and let go of her fear that he would eventually be out of her life. So simple to give him everything, she thought as she drifted on the wings of sweet release in his arms. So very easy to love him. To trust him, trust her heart. So very, very easy.

Rio shattered with a long shudder and another declaration of his love for her that she answered with one of her own. For the longest of moments they stayed united and even after their bodies parted, Joanna knew they would never be separated again. How she had ever lived without this special, spiritual unity, she didn't know. She'd never experienced it before, and she would never have it again with anyone but Rio Madrid.

She laid her head on his chest, contented to finally be at peace, to feel so certain about their love, hers and Joseph's future.

"I have some news." Rio's deep voice vibrated against Joanna's cheek.

"You want to make love again in record time?"

He chuckled. "That's a strong possibility, but this has to do with Allison Cartwright. I think I might know the father's identity."

Joanna raised her head and stared at him. "Lane Billings."

He looked surprised. "How did you know?"

She kissed the arch of his eyebrow and smoothed a hand over his face. "I ran into him in the NICU. He all but admitted it to me. How did you find out?"

"I was looking for you on the floor and he stopped me to ask how Allison was doing. I gave him a report and then he headed for her room, but not before saying something about making it up to her."

Joanna sighed and rested her face against Rio's chest once more, relishing the feel of his fingertips stroking her bare shoulder. "Allison's got a long road ahead of her and I'm hoping he'll be there for her. She's going to need him."

"I hope so, too. They're going to have a lot to deal with, but if they're lucky, they'll end up as happy as we are."

Joanna raised her head again and searched for any indecision in Rio's eyes. "Are you really happy?"

He painted kisses over her face. "Very happy. But you know what else would make me happy?"

She rubbed her hand down his belly and lower, surprised to find he was more than ready for action. "I bet I do."

Rio grinned then groaned. "That will definitely make me happy, and so would seeing you return to medical school to get your M.D. I could use a good partner. These hours are kicking my butt."

"Are you serious?"

"Yeah, I'm serious." He winked. "Would you like to check out my butt?"

"Sounds like fun." She reached beneath him and gave him a little pinch on one cheek. "So is that why you're marrying me, so you can have a readily available partner?''

''I'm marrying you so I can have a life partner, but I think you'd be a damned good OB.''

Joanna sat up and looked down on him. ''Rio, I hope you understand this, but I don't need an M.D. I'm happy being a midwife and I think there's a lot of honor in what I do.''

He reached up and touched her face. ''So do I, and in that case, I have an idea. We can take some of the colonel's money and open a not-for-profit birthing clinic. I'll keep my practice and you can run the place. I'll handle anything that needs to be handled at the hospital without charge. How does that sound?''

''Absolutely wonderful.'' She leaned down and kissed his lips. ''We'll make a great team, you and I.''

''We already do.'' He surveyed her with soft, loving eyes. ''And we'll hire plenty of staff, but while you're working to get things going, I can take care of Joseph, be a real dad to him. Get in some practice before we have kids of our own.''

''Ohmigosh, I forgot.'' Reaching over Rio, Joanna grabbed the cordless phone from the bedside table.

Rio sent a tantalizing fingertip down her bare back. ''What are you doing? Calling for pizza? I'm hungry for something else.''

Joanna batted his hand away from her breast as the phone began to ring. ''Patience, Doctor. We have plenty of time.''

''I like the way that sounds,'' Rio said.

When Joseph greeted her in his buoyant little-boy voice, Joanna's spirits lifted even more. ''Hi, sweetie, it's Mom. I have a surprise.'' As Rio sent her a heartfelt smile, as Joseph's excitement filtered through the line,

Joanna's heart soared with the infinite love she possessed for both her men.

"Joseph, honey, I've finally found you a dad."

* * * * *

COMING NEXT MONTH

#1501 TAMING THE BEASTLY MD—Elizabeth Bevarly
Dynasties: The Barones
When nurse Rita Barone needed a date for a party, she asked the very intriguing Dr. Matthew Grayson. Things heated up, and Rita wound up in Matthew's bed, where he introduced her to sensual delight. However, the next morning they vowed to forget their night of passion. But Rita couldn't forget. Could she convince the good doctor she needed his loving touch—*forever?*

#1502 INSTINCTIVE MALE—Cait London
Heartbreakers
Desperate for help, Ellie Lathrop turned to the one man who'd always gotten under her skin—enigmatic Mikhail Stepanov. Mikhail ignited Ellie's long-hidden desires, and soon she surrendered to their powerful attraction. But proud Mikhail wouldn't accept less than her whole heart, and Ellie didn't know if she could give him that.

#1503 A BACHELOR AND A BABY—Marie Ferrarella
The Mom Squad
Because of a misunderstanding, Rick Masters had lost Joanna Prescott, the love of his life. But eight years later, Rick drove past Joanna's house—just in time to save her from a fire and deliver her baby. The old chemistry was still there, and Rick fell head over heels for Joanna and her baby. But Joanna feared being hurt again; could Rick prove his love was rock solid?

#1504 TYCOON FOR AUCTION—Katherine Garbera
When Corrine Martin won sexy businessman Rand Pearson at a bachelor auction, she decided he would make the perfect corporate boyfriend. Their arrangement consisted of three dates. But Corrine found pleasure and comfort in Rand's embrace, and she found herself in unanticipated danger—of surrendering to love!

#1505 BILLIONAIRE BOSS—Meagan McKinney
Matched in Montana
He had hired her to be his assistant, but when wealthy Seth Morgan came face-to-face with beguiling beauty Kirsten Meadows, he knew he wanted to be more than just her boss. Soon he was fighting to persuade wary Kirsten to yield to him—one sizzling kiss at a time!

#1506 WARRIOR IN HER BED—Cathleen Galitz
Annie Wainwright had gone to Wyoming seeking healing, not romance. Then Johnny Lonebear stormed into her life, refusing to be ignored. Throwing caution to the wind, Annie embarked on a summer fling with Johnny that grew into something much deeper. But what would happen once Johnny learned she was carrying his child?

SDCNM0303